12 95

GOOD-BYE AND KEEP COLD

A Richard Jackson Book

Good-bye and Keep Cold

by JENNY DAVIS

ORCHARD BOOKS
A division of Franklin Watts, Inc.
New York • London

Orchard Books, 387 Park Avenue South, New York, New York
10016. Orchard Books Great Britain, 10 Golden Square, London
W1R 3AF England. Orchard Books Australia, 14 Mars Road, Lane
Cove, New South Wales 2066. Orchard Books Canada, 20 Torbay
Road, Markham, Ontario 23P 1G6.

Orchard B

Manufactured in the United States of An
Book design by Mina Greenstein
The text of this book is set in 12 pt. Garamond.
10 9 8 7 6 5 4 3 2 1

Library of Congress Cataloging-in-Publication Data
Davis, Jenny. Good-bye and keep cold.
   Summary: Edda's mother is courted by the man responsible for
her young father's death in a mine accident in a small Kentucky
town. [1. Family life—Fiction. 2. Kentucky—Fiction]
I. Title. PZ7.D2923Go 1987 [Fic] 87-5794
ISBN 0-531-05715-1 ISBN 0-531-08315-2 (lib. bdg.)

FOR MY CHILDREN

GOOD-BYE AND KEEP COLD

GOOD-BYE AND KEEP COLD

This saying good-bye on the edge of the dark
And the cold to an orchard so young in the bark
Reminds me of all that can happen to harm
An orchard away at the end of the farm
All winter, cut off by a hill from the house.
I don't want it girdled by rabbit and mouse,
I don't want it dreamily nibbled for browse
By deer, and I don't want it budded by grouse.
(If certain it wouldn't be idle to call
I'd summon grouse, rabbit, and deer to the wall
And warn them away with a stick for a gun.)
I don't want it stirred by the heat of the sun.
(We made it secure against being, I hope,
By setting it out on a northerly slope.)
No orchard's the worse for the wintriest storm;
But one thing about it, it mustn't get warm.
"How often already you've had to be told,
Keep cold, young orchard. Good-bye and keep cold.
Dread fifty above more than fifty below."
I have to be gone for a season or so.
My business awhile is with different trees,
Less carefully nurtured, less fruitful than these,
And such as is done to their wood with an ax—
Maples and birches and tamaracks.
I wish I could promise to lie in the night
And think of an orchard's arboreal plight
When slowly (and nobody comes with a light)
Its heart sinks lower under the sod.
But something has to be left to God.

ROBERT FROST

Chapter 1

When I was eight years old, my father died. He was blown up in a coal mine, on a mine really. A strip mine. People don't actually know how dangerous those are. You hear all the time about the deep mines, cave-ins and whatnot, but the strip jobs take their toll as well. I ought to know. My daddy's name was Ed Combs. He was twenty-nine years old. My name is Edda Combs; I was named after him, as you might have already suspicioned. We lived up on Cauley's Creek back then, over in Fincastle County, Kentucky.

I was home from school when the phone rang. Must have been about 3:30 or so. Mama and I were in the kitchen; she was cooking. Partly why I remember that day is because of what else happened at school, or else I remember what happened at school because of what happened to Daddy. I'm not sure which way it works. What happened at school was I had wet myself. I'd thought I was going to die, first from needing to go and then from shame, and I was telling Mama about it, since for one thing, she noticed right off the stain on the back of my green dress. And I was still smelling of it a little when I got to the house. I'd changed clothes; I hated wearing dresses anyway in those days. Put back on my jeans and some old shirt. I don't know what. What I do remember is sitting in the kitchen at the table and talking to her. I kept saying, "I don't *know* what happened," and she was saying, "Don't mind it, Edda; it happens to everybody now and then." It never did happen again to me, though it was close sometimes. (I made it all the way through grade school, and high school too, without ever once asking could I go to the bathroom.) Mama was cutting up carrots and potatoes and sliding me slices now and then across that yellow linoleum tabletop. It was September, and there was plenty of food just then from the garden.

And then the phone rang. She made a little face at me that was half grin and half irritation and went to answer it. It was the last real look she gave me for months. She didn't come back. The phone was out in the hallway, away from where I was sitting. I didn't listen, didn't hear her voice. I don't know what they said word for word, but the fact was Daddy'd been blown up and he was in the hospital. After I'd been sitting there a long time waiting for her to come back, I got bored and got up. I wandered into the front of the house and saw her tearing out the door, coattail flapping and her hair all over. She was a blur, just that, running out. I heard her say that Daddy was in the hospital and to be a good girl and that Banker was in charge. Banker was my great-uncle or my great-great-uncle or something.

He was old then, and he was real old last year when he died—eighty-nine. He lived with us for as long as I remember, although I was two when he moved in. But I can't go back any farther than three, and even then it's pretty hazy.

I went upstairs to Banker's bedroom. Jimmy was up there too. He's my brother, and at that time he was just a baby, sixteen months old. Jimmy and I have both figured out how old we were the day Daddy died. It was sort of like a game we played together after he got up in school and started fooling with numbers. He was one year, four months, and one week. I was eight years, three months, two weeks, and one day. Daddy didn't die that same day he got blown up. He lasted ten.

Banker was sitting up in his room just like always. His room was at the end of the house and had a slanty roof. It was the only room in the house that had wallpaper; everywhere else it was just paint and plaster or paneling. But in Banker's room it was wallpaper and real pretty too—roses on green vines crawling up all over in stripes. He had one big window, and it faced out over the creek. He had this little single bed covered with a quilt, and he made it up every day and changed his own sheets once a week. I brought him the clean ones, and he'd hand me out the dirty. He had a nice soft chair and a dresser, and all along one wall was a big rough-cut table. On that table, over it and under it too, were his newspaper cuttings. All over the place. When he died we went through his things and found twenty-seven suitcases full of clippings. Think about it. They were cataloged too, after a fashion. He had one called "Comedy" and one called "Tragedy" and one called "Godcalls" and on and on. There were clippings going back to 1922, and they covered all kinds of things. He took three newspapers back when we lived on Cauley's Creek and had himself a little reputation up at the store for being one smart, mysterious old buzzard.

Banker was sitting in his chair and holding Jimmy on his lap. I came in and stood beside them both for a minute, and then he shifted over, and all three of us were sitting in that chair together. Jimmy wasn't talking or even fooling around much. None of us were. We were just sitting, staring out in space. After a while Banker started patting my hair like he always did, and Jimmy started fussing. He was cutting teeth—forever, it seemed like—and crying a lot.

"Ed's been in a little accident," Banker said after a while.

"Daddy?" I asked, even though I knew that already from what the wind had blown back at Mama's leaving. I was trying not to have it so.

"She'll let us know," he said.

"What happened? Was it in the car?" There was a boy in my class at school whose big sister had been in a car accident.

"No, from what I gather, this was at work. Up on the job. Coal mining's nasty work, Edda, anyway you cut it."

"Is he okay, Banker? Do you think?"

"Dynamite it was. It won't hurt none to say your prayers."

I remember looking at him and thinking he was old. His face was so white, and it had a little white stubble on it, and his hair was white too, always hanging everywhere. His eyes were a pale watery blue, almost gray. He was in charge was what she'd said, I'd heard her. But Banker had only been downstairs one other time that I ever remembered, and that was when Mama broke her leg before Jimmy was born. I couldn't imagine how he was going to manage. Or me either.

Jimmy was crying, and I picked him up and told Banker I was going downstairs. He nodded at me and sat there stroking his chin like he was thinking. Jimmy was heavy—he was always a hefty kid and I was always a scrawny one—but I felt like carrying him. Besides, he wasn't too good on the steps yet. I wanted something to do. I felt so scared. I remember getting real dizzy when I started down the steps and thinking I might fall. The steps were steep and doubly dark because I'd been sitting in Banker's room staring out his one big window at the afternoon sun. Jimmy was wet and fidgety, and I swayed under him at the very top, but I held on. I leaned up against the wall and came down, one step at a time. Holding Jimmy made me keep going. That and knowing Mama wasn't home. I took him into the kitchen and gave him a Popsicle; I had one too. Then I sat back down at the table and looked at the potatoes and carrots Mama had been cutting. Everything was still there where we'd been sitting, just as we'd left it. There was a fly buzzing around, and I had the feeling it was a long, long time ago we'd been there, me telling her about how I wet myself in Miss Jenkins's room.

Jimmy was crawling around and pulling up on things. He could walk by then, but he preferred crawling most of the time. I kicked him his big swirly-patterned ball, and he started pounding on it, saying, "Ball, ball." After a while Banker came down. He stood there for a minute at the other end of the kitchen just blinking his eyes and getting used to it. That kitchen was like a big long hallway, with the table where I was at one end, and the doorway, where he was standing, at the other. I don't even know if he could see me. He was seventy-five that day (and three months and five days) and couldn't see too well due to cataracts. He used a magnifying glass to read the newspapers with, and I don't know if he could see far off at all.

It was strange to see him in the kitchen. I wasn't used to it. I really hadn't seen him stand up that much, and he looked funny that way, smaller than when he was sitting down.

"Hey, Banker," I said to him, to let him know I was there. Jimmy had crawled over to him and was hanging on his legs.

"Hey, Edda," he called out as if over a great distance. Which it was, in a way. "If you hold Jimmy boy here, I'll see what I can do about some supper. How's that sound?"

It sounded good to me. So Banker took charge, like Mama expected. He was funny in the kitchen, always dropping stuff and making mistakes and then saying, "Well, well, what have I done?" Sometimes grown-ups make mistakes on purpose so little kids will feel good when they catch them out. My daddy used to do that. He'd be reading me a story and he'd say "cat" instead of "dog," and then he'd act tickled when I caught him. Like I was wonderful. But the mistakes Banker was making were for real. He didn't know where anything was, and he didn't know how to cook. I didn't either. We had peanut butter and jelly sandwiches that night, and orange juice. The orange juice was frozen. Banker got it out and opened it up and just looked at it. Then he took a spoonful of it and put it in a cup and ran some water on it. He stirred it up and gave it to Jimmy. We both knew that wasn't what orange juice usually looked like—this brew was light and watery—but Jimmy drank it up and put his little pudgy fist down in the cup to fish out the blob of frozen stuff that was still there. Banker plopped me a spoonful of it in a glass, and I told him to skip the water. I have ever since been partial to eating it like that, straight out of the can, with a spoon. It's good.

He just left the carrots and potatoes sitting there on the table while we ate. Banker and I both ate some carrots. He wouldn't let me give one to Jimmy even though he cried for it. "No, no," he said to Jimmy. "You're too young for that, little fella." To me he said, "I read about this just last month. There was a baby up in Louisville, I believe it was, choked on a carrot. He's too little for that." Fact is, Jimmy was choking on the peanut butter. I didn't think Mama ever gave it to him before, but I had no idea what she did give him so I didn't say anything. He kept balling up the bread in his fist and squishing it around until it came out between his fingers, and then he'd lick it off and sort of gag when he swallowed. Pretty disgusting, but what can you expect? He was a baby.

Banker and I were both waiting for the phone to ring. Which it did not. I went into the living room and watched TV. Nobody said not to, and it felt so good to just lie down in there on the couch and watch "The Beverly Hillbillies." Mama always said it was a terrible show because hillbillies *obviously* really weren't like that. She hated stereotyping. Even in the third grade I knew words like that. Mama was college educated—Daddy too—and she in particular didn't believe in talking down to children. She said what she thought to whoever was listening—which, when I was little, was often me. Daddy may have been like that too, but it's harder to remember with him.

Banker came in and asked did I know where any diapers were. That I did know. I wasn't much for cooking, but Mama had put me to work a long time ago changing diapers. I went upstairs and got what I needed and changed Jimmy there on the couch. Banker was sitting in a chair watching the show and never said word one about it. I don't think he cared whether I watched "The Beverly Hillbillies" or not. He didn't care about stereotyping, or if he did, he never said so.

When it was over and the song went off, he said, "Is it time for you to go to bed?" It was 7:30, and I didn't have to go to bed on a school night till 8:00, but for some reason I didn't argue with him. "Can I help you?" he asked.

"No, Banker, I can do it." I wasn't thinking about taking a bath or brushing my teeth or anything I might do if Mama was there. "Do you think he's okay?" I asked him.

"Edda," he said and then didn't say any more. Maybe he couldn't think of what else to say. He just said my name, like that was some kind of answer.

"Well, good night, Banker," I said when I realized he had nothing else to say.

"Good night, Peachpit," he murmured. For some reason that was his nickname for me. He only used it now and then.

I took Jimmy up with me. His crib was in my room. He was wearing only a diaper and a T-shirt, and he often slept like that so I just hauled him in. He was babbling a lot, and I thought I heard him say "Dadda" and "Mama," so I all of a sudden started talking to him. I told him everything that was happening as far as I understood it. He was standing up, holding onto the bars on his crib, just looking at me. At first, when I started talking, he got excited and started babbling louder and faster, but after a while—he may have somehow caught the gist of what I was saying or it may have been my tone—he got real quiet and just watched me. I was walking up and down in front of him, pulling off my shirt and jeans and changing into my nightgown, all the time talking. It was a mistake, talking like that. It made it all so suddenly real I couldn't take it back like I'd been doing inside my head all evening. Now it was really happening, and I had even said so. Daddy was lying there at the hospital, and he was blown up. I started crying. Shortly thereafter Jimmy started crying too, and I picked him up and took him into bed with me.

I must have laid there half the night. I kept thinking about Daddy being in the hospital. I'd been up there when Mama broke her leg. She was pregnant then, and she'd been climbing up on some chair to get something out of the top of the closet. She'd started to sway and then tumbled off and started panting like a dog and moaning. I was six then, and I'd been sitting on the bed watching the whole thing. She finally managed to convince me to go get Banker. Daddy was at work. Banker made a phone call, and before you know it, Daddy was there. He picked Mama up like she was hardly any weight at all and laid her in the back of his truck. She was crying and laughing at the same time, and he kept kissing her on the forehead and all over her face, telling her to hush. He told me to get in front, and we drove her to the hospital. I remember that place. These men in white suits came out running and put her on a stretcher. She was crying all the time by then and saying, "I'm bleeding, I'm bleeding." Later I found out that she was worried about the baby and not her leg, but at first I thought it was her leg that was gushing all that blood.

Daddy left me sitting on those plastic chairs all hooked together side by each. It was a waiting room. After a while he came back and sat down too, but he couldn't keep still.

He kept walking all around that room, and I just sat there following him with my eyes. They kept her overnight and set her leg. In the morning the doctor found out she was still pregnant and told her it was a miracle. Daddy took me up to see her in a room with three other people in it. One of them had tubes running into her nose. A nurse came in and said I wasn't allowed to be there, so Daddy told me to go wait in the hall. Mama saw me and waved.

There's a way things sound in the hospital that's like nowhere else I've ever been. People talk kind of soft, but it seems to come out loud. Windows don't open in those rooms, and all the time there's the noise of wheels and metal things rattling on trays. Now Daddy was up there in the midst of it.

I prayed as best I could that night, but it didn't sound right. At one point I snuck downstairs and saw Banker asleep, stretched out on the couch. I think he wanted to be downstairs in case the phone rang. Which it did not. I got the whole box of vanilla wafers out of the cupboard in the kitchen and tiptoed back up. Jimmy and I ate every one of them that night.

I finally did go to sleep, and when I woke up it was almost morning. Jimmy was slapping on my face with his hand. He wasn't being mean about it, just trying to get me up. There was a gray, heavy light outside, not daylight yet but getting there. I felt gritty-eyed and confused. Jimmy's diaper was leaking, and we were both kind of sticky and wet. First thing I did was go look in Mama and Daddy's room, but of course they weren't in there. The bed was just the same as yesterday. Jimmy was right behind me. "Mama? Dadda?" he asked, and this time he said it plain so there was no mistaking.

"Sshh," I told him and took him back into our room, where I changed his diaper. I had a terrible knot in my stomach, so bad it was almost hard to breathe. Jimmy and I just fooled around in there for a while. I did wash my face and put on some school clothes, but I couldn't imagine going to school. When it got a little lighter outside, I took Jimmy and we went downstairs. Banker was still asleep on the couch. His mouth was hanging open, and he was making little noises, like grunts.

Jimmy, soon as I put him down, went over and started pulling on Banker's face. He woke up and looked at us like, where am I? I was feeling about like that myself. I could tell Mama hadn't called, and I didn't know what it meant. Banker turned on the TV, and we watched the farm report.

"Great thing, television," Banker said to me. "Think about it, Edda. It's all out there, coming into your own damn living room." Banker was all the time swearing. Mama gave up trying to get him to quit, and none of us ever did take it up much, although Jimmy, when he was six years old and had just had his mouth washed out with soap for saying something, said that when he grew up he was going to write a book called "I Love to Cuss." Banker's mouth was filthy. A garbage can, Mama called it, but then she'd smile. Anyway, he had this thing about television.

He hardly ever watched it back then. He didn't have one in his room, and he hardly ever, as I said, came down. But he thought it was a wonderful invention. On Cauley's Creek we got exactly two channels. That's it. And we were lucky to get those, living as far out as we did. Mama was all the time telling us what we could watch and what we couldn't and how too much TV would rot our minds and did we want to be simpletons. But Banker thought it was something special. For the last three years before he died he had a little TV in his room, and he watched the thing day and night. Had he known about those VCRs, he would have no doubt been clipping TV the way he did newspapers.

Well, that morning we sat there and watched it. We didn't know what else to do, for one thing. It seemed to me that the world had stopped its course, that everyone, every*thing* was holding its breath and had been since the phone first rang the day before. None of us seemed to be hungry, although at some point I do remember Banker and I went and fixed bowls of cereal. We brought them into the living room to eat in front of the TV, which was an unheard of thing to do. But then, it was all unheard of.

And then, finally, about 8:00, Mama came home. Jimmy and I jumped up and ran over to her. She looked strange, real black-eyed and tired but fired up, intense. She didn't hug us or talk to us or act in any way like Mama. Banker was the only one who hadn't moved when she opened the door. He was still sitting on the couch. She stood there in the middle of the living room, staring out over our heads, staring maybe at Banker, maybe at Bugs Bunny, which was on. Finally Banker spoke.

"Frances? Frances, what's your news? Come sit down here. Edda, turn that thing off." He waved me toward the television, which I clicked off. Quiet seemed to land with a thud. Mama just kept standing there, staring. She had her head cocked a little as though she was listening to something we couldn't hear. I found out later that she was. "Frances?" Banker said again.

"Ed's bad, Banker. Bad." Her voice didn't sound right. It came out high and squeaky, and Mama's voice was always real low.

"How bad, Fran?"

"Bad."

"Mama! Mama!" Jimmy started in tugging at her skirt. She looked down at him and me too. She reached out a hand to each of us and we took it. I thought I was going to cry, but instead I just stood there on one side of her and Jimmy on the other holding her hands. She kept looking over to where Banker sat, but I don't think she was looking at him.

"I'll take Edda to school," she said finally. Her words came out real slow. "She's missed the bus. Jimmy I'll take to Annie's house. You take the bus home and walk over and get him, okay?" She said this last to me, and I nodded yes. I was profoundly relieved that she seemed to have some sort of plan.

She went upstairs then, and I could hear water running in the bathroom. Banker and I cleared up the bowls and spoons from the living room. The potatoes were still on the kitchen table. They'd turned a streaky brown where they'd been cut. The carrots we'd finished at dinner. I opened the back door and started pitching potatoes out into the yard. I hated those potatoes. I wanted them dead, gone, out of my sight, out of our house. When I finished, I turned around and practically bowled Banker over. I hadn't realized he was so close up behind me. He reached out his withered old hand to pat my head, but I ducked under him and got away. I didn't want anyone to be nice to me just then; I was afraid I couldn't bear it.

Chapter 2

Annie's house was about a mile from ours. She lived up near the mouth of Cauley's Creek, by the store. Annie and Mama were good friends, best friends I guess. Neither one of them was from Kentucky, and that gave them some sort of bond. Also, they were about the same age, and to my mind they looked like they could have been sisters, only Mama was taller by far and much darker. Annie had come to Fincastle County with her husband, Irv. They had both come as VISTA workers, out to fight poverty and whatnot in Appalachia. But then Irv left—left, as I understood it (which was not much), with another woman. And Annie stayed. She taught an art class up at the high school, but only part-time. Mama always teased her that that was a crazy way to fight hunger, what with all the starving artists already out there. Annie would just laugh and shrug her shoulders. She was from up in Detroit or California or someplace and had a lot of money, or so I heard rumored.

Lots of times, especially after Irv left, Annie would spend whole days, and sometimes the night, over at our house.

I'd come down in the morning, and there she'd be on the couch. She'd call me over, and I'd snuggle in with her under the blankets. She smelled like woodsmoke and pine all mixed up, and she had the shortest hair I ever saw on a woman. She wore big glasses that made her look owlish, but in the mornings, when we'd snuggle, she'd squint at everything. Even me, and I was right next to her. After Mama broke her leg, Annie moved in for a whole week and just took over. She made it seem like a party. Daddy was always laughing at her jokes, and back then it seemed like they could make a joke out of thin air. Annie was fun. I'm sorry everything got so messed up and horrible later on because we never saw her after that.

That morning, in the car, I held Jimmy in my lap. Mama and I didn't say a word to each other as we drove down to Annie's. I was glad to have Jimmy to squeeze; and the more I'd squeeze, the more he'd squirm, so I was occupied. Irv and Annie had bought the oldest, shabbiest-looking house on the creek. It sat back from the road in a little yard that backed up onto the mountain, so it seemed enclosed. It was a real old-timey type of cabin—"real log," Annie used to say, as if that was a very good thing. I remember Daddy saying that only VISTA people would want to live in a place like that. They had to fetch water from the well and use an outhouse for a bathroom. Inside, the place was all torn up from where Irv had started to make repairs before he left but never finished. It was just one huge room downstairs and another one up. Annie was no hand at all with carpentry, and for a long time after Irv had gone she just lived in his wake, stepping over half-sawed planks and lifting wires out of the way. Their idea of fixing it up was to bring it down to its bones and add a bathroom. They already had electricity. That morning, when we pulled up, Annie came out on the porch. She'd been crying. Behind her big owl glasses her eyes were red and puffy.

Mama took Jimmy up on the porch and set him down. She and Annie hugged each other for what seemed a long time. Mama was shaking her head back and forth, and Annie's hand was kind of beating time on her back. When they quit, Annie looked down at me and waved. I smiled back as best I could.

"I'll see you this afternoon, Edda," she called.

Mama got back in the car and drove me to school. She reached out once and patted me on my leg, but then she took her hand away and kept driving.

School was in town, Spence, which was about four miles down the new road from Cauley's Creek. Spence isn't much of a town, but it did have a stoplight, the hospital, and my school. Course it had stores too, a few of them anyway, and it was actually the county seat, but that doesn't mean much. Mama pulled into the school parking lot and turned off the engine. Classes had already started, and there wasn't anyone around. I was scared to move, and Mama didn't make any sign for me to go. We just sat there.

"I'm going to need a note," I told her. I had seen what happened to kids who came in late, and I knew that much.

"I'll go in with you," she said, but she made no move.

"Is Daddy going to die?" I asked by mistake. It was a terrible question. I hadn't meant to ask it. I didn't want to know.

"He might." I felt my stomach start to churn, and I was thinking I might throw up. "You're going to have to help out, Edda. I know you can do it. Help Banker and Annie with Jimmy, okay?"

"I will, Mama."

"I know you will, darling. I know you will." She still didn't sound like herself, and even though she was talking to me I kept thinking she wasn't. "Daddy's hurt bad, Edda. We just have to see."

We got out of the car and went into the school. She knew the way to Miss Jenkins's room. Walking with her down that still hallway, I noticed she was limping. She always did limp a little after she broke her leg, but that day it seemed more pronounced. We passed the bathroom and she stopped. "Why don't you go right now," she said, and I knew then that she had not forgotten me completely. I ducked in and emptied myself as much as I could. My stomach still hurt.

When we went into Miss Jenkins's room, everybody looked up. I sidled into my desk just as quick as I could while Mama went over and said a few words, in a very low voice, to the scariest woman in the United States. Miss Jenkins looked over at me and nodded once to Mama, still fixing her eagle eye on me. I looked down and Mama left. Miss

Jenkins put a stack of worksheets in front of me, and I got busy.

It was ten days, as I know for a fact, before Daddy died. Every day, except on the weekend, I'd stop at Annie's and pick up Jimmy. Sometimes she'd drive me home; sometimes Jimmy and I would walk, which is very slow going with a child that age. Banker stayed at home; he was always there, up in his room, after that first day and night. Annie brought food up and sometimes stayed to put Jimmy and me to bed. Mama came in every morning and changed clothes. Then back she went to the hospital, to sit at Daddy's bed.

Annie told me what was what. Daddy was unconscious, which she said was like sleeping only more so. He was in a tent—a plastic tent, she said—and there were machines hooked up on his skin and in his mouth. She said he wasn't feeling any pain. I wonder to this day if that was so.

Mama told me later that those machines made a noise, a breathing sort of a noise and a steady *beep-beep*. It was that sound she was listening to for all those days. Even when she wasn't with him, which wasn't much, she could hear it in her mind, *whish-whoosh, beep-beep*. When he died, it was a Sunday and Mama was home, taking out a little time to wash the dishes. She turned off the water real sudden and tilted her head toward the window in front of the sink. Then she turned around, and I saw her face crumple, just collapse in on itself; and before I knew it she was gone out the door, and I could hear the car starting up outside. The sound had stopped in her mind, and just like that she knew

for certain he was gone. Sure enough, that day she didn't stay all day and all night. She was back within an hour, and Annie was with her.

"Daddy's dead, Edda." She told it to me real fast, as she was still coming in the door. Then she knelt down or squatted somehow so that I reached the top of her head. She put her arms around me, and we both started crying. Annie, I believe, picked up Jimmy and took him upstairs to tell Banker. Mama took me over to the couch, and I sat for a long, long time in her lap. I didn't want to stop crying because I knew if I did, she would put me down, and I was afraid if she did that she might die too, might disappear. I cried till I got the hiccups, and then I cried a little more. Mama's face was streaked with tears, but she wasn't sobbing the way I was, just leaking. After a while she went upstairs and went to bed. It was the first time in ten days she'd rested in her own bed.

Banker and Annie and Jimmy came downstairs. Annie made phone calls, and Banker turned on the TV, but there were only preachers on (being a Sunday), and he turned it off. I went outside. The house seemed too small to hold me just then; I had to get out. Daddy and I had a place across the creek and up a way that we called Heaven. With him dead and all, the name bothered me a little, but that was what he called it when he was still alive, Heaven. There was a little tiny waterfall there and some flat rocks. It was full of pine and rhododendron, some hardwoods too, which that afternoon, September 30, were just beginning to turn.

I picked my way down there, feeling blind. I was acting blind too because I kept bumping into things and stumbling over roots. When I got to Heaven, I lay down in some pine needles. They were soft and prickly both, and the ground was cool. I watched the water splashing down and gliding over those flat rocks, looking like glass. Suddenly there were birds screaming overhead, loud, horrible screams, like people in pain. I started screaming back at them: "Shut up! Shut up!" I was yelling, just as loudly as I could. These were forbidden words; we were more likely to get in trouble for saying "shut up" than for cussing, but I didn't care. Mama was sleeping in her dark room up at the house, and Daddy was dead. There was no one to stop me, and that in itself made it all the more frightening and necessary to do.

Chapter 3

The next few days saw more people and food in that house than had ever been there before. The rooms seemed to billow out with people, all of them talking. I wove between stomachs and around backs, under cigarettes and flat into bosoms, clasped to I don't know how many chests. Jimmy was hard to keep up with, and he was my job. The kitchen, that long, narrow trestle of a room, was lined, sometimes with men, passing drinks and smoking, and sometimes with women, smoking too maybe and filling cups and plates. The women moved around more than the men and fed us better, but any time of the day or night for those two days before Daddy was put in the ground, that kitchen was a fearful wonder to traverse. Personally, I could have done with staying out of there, but Jimmy was the one—he kept dragging me in or being there when I was looking for him. For one thing, he wanted to be close to the food. And for another, he's easier being around people than I am. Jimmy's the kind of person they probably invented wakes for: he takes comfort from his fellows. I imagine Daddy was that kind too; he certainly had a lot of people come to pay their respects. But Mama didn't care for it and neither did I.

I could tell she didn't because she just sat there on the living room couch for two days and looked at everybody. Somebody would lean over and say, "Taste this pie, now, Frances," or "I know Ed would be proud at how many people are here," and Mama would look deep into the person's eyes but not nod or speak back or anything. It was like she was looking for someone, real slow, like under water, and if you weren't it, she looked on.

I know I didn't like it because there was no room to breathe in that house, no place to go. There were cousins I never saw before and didn't much care for in my room. People's coats and bags and things were everywhere. I kept running outside, down to the creek or up the road a piece, just to get away. On the last day before we went to the church, I thought of Banker's room. He had let no one come in and kept the door locked the whole time. I crept in when he was out to the bathroom, shut the door, and for a few moments before he came back, I was alone.

When Banker did come back and saw me, he let me stay. It was restful in there. You could hear the mumble from the house down below and all around, but in those gabled walls the air seemed still and quiet. "Whatcha been doing?" I asked him. He'd sat down at his table and was holding scissors and newspaper.

"Mostly I've been praying, about your dad, and . . . you, and . . . all. What about you? How's it going?"

"Okay, I guess." I was sitting in his big chair and swinging my legs. "Banker, what do people really mean when they say that? How's what going?" I'd been wanting to get this cleared up for a long time, and Banker was just the man to do it.

"It just means, uh, I see you're not down on the floor kicking and screaming, so hello. It's just a way to take up space when you're having a conversation with someone. Now, Edda, you know that." He cast me a suspicious look, like was I pulling his leg or what? But then he hadn't been downstairs for two days, wandering in and out of people who, every one them, asked that: How's it going? How are you doing? Doing what?

I didn't want to talk, and I think Banker sensed that. We were both quiet, he with his cutting and reading and I looking out his window. It was a mild day, but it had been cold and raw the day before. Changeable weather meant something; I'd heard somebody downstairs say so. The bank leading up from the creek was brown and wet-looking. Up high I could see the treetops and the cloudy blue sky. And then what? Heaven? Is that where my father went? I wanted to know. (I'd still like to know.) Where was he? I didn't want him to be up in heaven watching me if we couldn't talk. For eight years I had talked to my father; I couldn't stand to not hear his voice again.

And then too, I was still hearing his voice, not like Mama heard that beeper, but memories of it. They were still strong after two weeks. "Edda, shut the door" was the last thing he'd said to me in his life. He hollered it out to me actually because, leaving for school in a hurry, I'd forgotten to push the sticky screen door all the way into place. I had to go back and kick it shut.

I could hear him calling me out in the mornings: "Come on, honey, time to get up." Easy as could be, I could still hear him saying that. Daddy's voice was like gravel, but when he was happy, especially if he was laughing, heh-heh, it had a musical quality to it. Singing rocks. It's hard to describe. Back then I could still hear it plain, and I was still listening to it. Later what hurt so much was when I realized I couldn't make him say anything new. I could imagine what he might say, but that's not the same thing. Ed Combs was gone. His piece was said forever and all time.

Jimmy was the one who led me straight into Henry John Fitzpatrick. It was bedtime on the second day. I'd been fortified by my time with Banker but was feeling a little panicky because of how many hours had slipped away in there. I heard Annie calling for me and Banker did too. He pulled the lock on his door and let me out. "You're a good girl, Peachpit," he told me. Annie wanted me to go kiss Mama good night. "And where's Jimmy?" she wanted to know.

I knocked on Mama's door, which felt funny, but I'd seen people do it in the last two days and felt like maybe I should too. She was sitting on their bed, combing out her hair. Mama's hair was long and black and wavy. It was like hair you see on TV commercials, but I know for a fact she never used anything special on it. She looked at me hard when I came in, and I could tell right off I wasn't the one she was waiting for. She looked away. "I'm tired, Edda. I'm going to bed. Annie said she'll help you get Jimmy down. Okay?"

"Uh-huh."

"Tomorrow is the funeral. Do you know that?"

"Yes."

"Do you know what a funeral is, baby?"

"I reckon I do. Daddy's going to be buried, right?"

"That's right, something like that. But he's not in the box, Edda. Remember that, hear?"

"What box?"

"There's a box there, a coffin. That's what they put in the ground." Mama shuddered and held her arms out to me. I crawled into her lap. I could feel her hair teasing down on my neck. "Daddy's not in there, not anymore."

"Where is he, Mama?"

"I can't say for sure. I wish I could. But what's in that box, in that coffin, are just his earthly remains. It's not really your daddy. Do you understand that?"

"I guess so," I lied.

"If I know your daddy, he's probably out on the mountain somewhere, looking things over. And probably, somehow, don't ask me all the details, he's going to go be with God. This burying—it's just what's left for us to do. I don't want you to be scared about it."

"Will I sit with you?" What few times we had ever been

to church before this I ended up downstairs in the nursery with the babies. I didn't want to do that again.

"Yes, girl, you'll sit with me. Is that what you want?"

"Uh-huh, I do."

"And so you shall. Now go round up Jimmy and let's get some sleep. That bunch down there . . ." She made a gesture with her hand, an empty, lopsided half-circle. I kissed her good night and left her in there, combing out her hair.

Downstairs was still full. I bumped and nudged my way through the living room and into the kitchen. There were women by the sink, washing up. Annie was there, blowing blue smoke and leaning up against the cabinet, not working. She reached over and pulled me into her hip, scrunching my face against the stiff material of her shirtwaist.

"Have you eaten?" she asked.

I had eaten so much the first day and a half that missing supper that night had not mattered. I wasn't hungry. The smell of ham and cooked beans was beginning to make me sick. Even the cakes didn't tempt me just then. I told her yes and she nodded absently. Either she didn't care or she understood.

"Jimmy's here somewhere. Why don't you round him up and I'll see you both to bed," she said.

I unhooked my head from her arm and edged my way down the kitchen. There were men sitting at the table, and more men hunkered down against the wall. I didn't see Jimmy.

I let myself out the back door. The screen didn't shut all the way, but Daddy wasn't there to holler me back to fix it right and I didn't. It was dark out by then, and I couldn't see much at first, but I heard Jimmy's voice, babbling away, not far. I stepped out into the yard, away from the house lights and looked for him, following the sound of his voice. I heard another voice too, a deep mumble of a sound. I couldn't make out any words.

Over by the coal shed I finally found him, found both of them. They had Mrs. Roosevelt, our cat, with them, and the man was jerking a string up and down, making her dance. He was sitting on the big stump that Daddy used for chopping wood. Jimmy was clapping his hands and bouncing up and down on his little fat legs. He was saying, "Cat! Cat!" When I came up to them, the man dropped the string and Jimmy dove at my legs, hugging me. I picked him up and held him on my hip.

"Hey," I said politely to the man.

"Hello," he answered. "You must be Edda."

"Yessir, I am." I could barely make his face out in the darkness, but I saw that he had a mustache and the saddest-looking eyes I'd ever seen on a human being. Only time I ever saw eyes anywhere like his was on this poor old mangy hound dog that had been up at the school bus stop one day, up by the store. I practiced all day things to say to talk Mama and Daddy into letting me keep it, but when I got back that afternoon, it was lying dead and full of flies in the middle of the new road. Mama always said the dumbest dogs in the world lived in eastern Kentucky, but then Daddy would say they were the smartest ones because all the dumb ones get killed. Natural selection and whatnot. That's what his eyes reminded me of, that dumb dog.

"I'm Henry John Fitzpatrick," he said. "I worked with your dad."

"Oh." I couldn't think of much else to say. How's it going? How you doing? It was true he wasn't lying down screaming in the dirt, but I wasn't too sure he was far from it, what with those eyes and all. And it was more than that. He treated me real seriously, kind of like Banker did. I could tell he wasn't about to chuck me under the chin or pinch my cheek. So I didn't want to talk down to him, like I did to some people who talked down to me.

"Is your mama still up?"

"No. She went to bed."

"Yeah, it's getting kind of late. I expect we'll be going soon too."

Jimmy started squirming so I set him down. He toddled over to Henry John Fitzpatrick and pounded on his thighs. "That means he wants to get up," I told him. He looked at me real blankly for a second. "On your lap," I explained. "He's not one bit shy. Maybe you figured that out by now."

Henry John smiled and looked down at Jimmy. He put his hands over Jimmy's where they were pounding on him. Jimmy looked up, right straight into his eyes. Henry John flinched just a little and then picked him up like he was made of fine china. Whatever Jimmy's made of it's not fine china, nor anything else the least bit fragile, but that's how he held him, like he was afraid he might break. Even when Jimmy started pawing at his face and pulling on his mustache, he held himself real still, hardly breathing. I just stood there and watched.

From the house a man called, "Henry John? It's time. Let's go." I heard it plain, and I know he did too, but he never made a move. He sat there looking at Jimmy with those sad, sad eyes, holding him so carefully while Jimmy pulled his face this way and that.

"Sir?" I said at last, stepping up to take Jimmy.

"He's a fine boy, isn't he?"

"Yessir, he is. We all think so." I reached over and pulled him off the man's lap. He flinched again, ever so slightly.

"Edda," he said, "I'm sorry, so sorry, about what happened to your dad." He wasn't looking at me, just shaking his head and talking to the ground.

I didn't say anything back to that. There wasn't much to say, and I'd been saying what there was for two days now; I'd had my fill of manners. I looked up at the moon which was huge.

"Look here, mister. It's a harvest moon for sure," I said. In some way I was trying to comfort him. He looked up at it too. There were stars out by now; it was a beautiful night.

"I better go," he said at last and pulled himself up. He walked like an old man, like Banker, I thought. So slow and sort of stooped. But he wasn't old or at least not like that. He was about Daddy's age I guessed. And Mama's.

He went back into the house, and after a while I heard doors slamming and cars starting up. I stayed out there with Jimmy and Mrs. Roosevelt, who'd come up to get petted on. I showed Jimmy the moon, but I don't know if he really saw it. After a while Annie came out and put us to bed.

Chapter 4

The next day we got up early and ate breakfast, just Jimmy and Mama and I. We took Banker up a tray, same as ever: prune juice, soft-boiled egg, and toast; coffee later. Mama said we'd leave at 10:00. Banker said he'd be ready. My cousins were still sleeping, three of them, like logs in a row across the foot of my room. My Uncle Jack was on the couch and Ida, his wife, was somewhere. I don't know where exactly, maybe down at Annie's. I believe late sleeping ran in their family, but it didn't in ours.

And just as well for Jimmy and me. I missed Mama about as much as I did Daddy, and in some way it was even scarier having her be there and be so strange than it was to have Daddy gone altogether. I didn't realize then that dead meant for such a long time. And Mama *was* there, at least some.

That morning she kissed us both and carried Jimmy around while she put out our food. She sat down with us as we ate, nursing her big white mug of coffee. She was drinking it straight that morning—she always did—and looking deep into the cloudy blackness. She'd put her nose down close to her cup and take a deep breath and look up, seeing nothing or else I don't know what. She had lines in her face that had never been there before. Her eyes were strange and sad, very dark that day. "I don't feel good, you all," she told us. Jimmy and I both knew it. He kept catching her eye and putting on a big smile, like "Hi, it's me!" real loving; and she'd smile back at him but be looking away.

Mama was present, if unaccounted for. Daddy really wasn't there at all. His chair was there at the table, the place he always sat in the mornings. The air that his body would have taken up was there—we all glanced into it often enough to know that—but he wasn't. I ate raisin bran and told Mama about the new way to eat orange juice Banker and I had discovered. She said. "Oh," "Um," "Uh-huh," but I could tell she wasn't listening. Pretty soon the other people woke up and we got ready to go.

The funeral was really horrible. I can't think of any other way to put it. Mama had insisted on a closed casket, and a lot of people were put out about it. It's custom up there to leave the casket open. Some people felt unable to say good-bye without seeing the body. But Mama had said no. It wasn't to be done at the service. Some of the relatives on Daddy's side insisted, and she'd said they could come look at him beforehand but not during the service. What I saw, and I sat in the front row, was a big brown box with lots of flowers on it. There was also a flag draped over it because Daddy had been a veteran.

Personally, I didn't really much want to see him dead.

It seemed spooky to me, and I was afraid of what he might look like. I would rather have seen him, if not for the last time hollering at me from the kitchen table, then in the hospital like Mama did. I would have liked that transitional image. What I had was here and gone. That, and a lot of people in the house.

I don't know what that preacher said, but it scared me nearly to death. I mean it. He was the kind that slobbered when he got real excited, and he was excited something terrible that day. His voice, I remember, was screechy and booming both. He pointed his finger at people. I got the shivers, and my teeth started to chatter. By the time it was over my bones were rattling.

Banker led me out of there and put his handsome blue suit jacket over my shoulders as we walked up to the grave-yard. A lot of dead in eastern Kentucky are buried facing a sunrise, up on a hillside. My daddy is.

Most people were screaming and crying. Jimmy was, for one, but he wasn't the only one by a long shot. I still remember people's cries bouncing off the wooden walls of that church, and then later on the path up to where he was put in the ground. It sounded again like those birds I'd screamed at, but I didn't tell any people to shut up or even feel like saying it. The crying and carrying on was hard to take, but there was some kind of comfort in it too. My mother didn't scream or cry out. She leaked tears as she would leak them for years to come. I shook. Jimmy howled. And Banker just stood there.

I'm glad we didn't stay to hear too many of those rocks

pounding on the coffin's lid. I felt like jumping down there and throwing back the clumps of dirt and the rocks, felt like stopping the whole show and saying, "Allee, allee in free. You win, Daddy. You can come out now." But we didn't stay. Mama picked up Jimmy and gave him a teething biscuit out of her purse. With Banker's hand guiding me firmly by the neck, we walked away. We were the first ones down the hill, and we got straight in our car; Mama drove us home. And then she went to bed and stayed there for four days.

Banker made me and Jimmy get in a big hot tub of water and soak. After that we wandered around until Annie got us. We stayed down at her house most of the time the next few days. She clucked a lot over me and kept feeling my forehead. I didn't have to go to school till the next week. Annie's house was okay except for two main things: the outhouse, and watching Jimmy in the midst of all those wires and nails and jagged edges.

The outhouse stank. But what I really hated about it was the snakes. It was all viny and overgrown out there, and the building itself sat up on irregular stone blocks, a perfect place for snakes to nest in. Every time I'd go out there, I'd hear something slithery in the underbrush, and it gave me the shivers all over again. Irv, I remember, had shot a copperhead in their front yard one time, and both he and Annie acted like it was a big accomplishment to have snakes. I guess they felt they were properly one of the gang then.

Jimmy was into everything he could see. I wanted to be

home, but we were being kept out of there because Mama needed her rest. Annie tried to talk about Daddy, but it made me uncomfortable to hear her. "Your dad had a mighty fine sense of humor," she would say, or "I bet he's mad about this. I know I am." I never knew what to say to her when she would get in her confiding moods.

From Annie I learned that somebody had blown a charge too soon, something went screwy, the signals were crossed, and Daddy'd got caught in the middle. That somebody was Henry John Fitzpatrick. I thought: So that's who blew Daddy up. Him. I didn't hold it against him at first. I just thought, Oh, it was him. Impersonal, kind of, like a marksman before he pulls the trigger. Annie knew a lot of things, and she liked to talk. The rest of the time she would go and lock herself up in the loft, which was her bedroom and her painting studio. Good light and all that. Which left me watching Jimmy on my own. I can see now it was too big a job for an eight-year-old girl.

I don't *know* what else I was doing that one day when I was supposed to be watching him. I can't remember. All I heard was his cry, strangled, choked in his throat. I turned in time to see him get a jolt of electricity high enough to throw him through the air. He lay in a heap; there was a smell of burning. I picked my way across the room to him. He was behind a big stack of lumber and a circular saw. Up on the wall was an unfinished plug. I'd told him two hundred times or more, "No, Jimmy, not over there." You think I'm exaggerating? I'm not. He went over there anyway when I wasn't watching, and now he was a heap on the floor. I started screaming.

By the time Annie registered the sounds and started down the steps, Jimmy was coming to. He didn't cry at first but made motions, and I could see he was alive. I stopped screaming and started crying, blubbering big as anything. I slobbered all over him, hugging him and crying; he started crying too once he caught his breath. By the time Annie got to us we were both crying hard. She saw his finger was burned, right at the tip, and the smell was still in the air. She must have measured in her mind how far he was jolted. Pretty soon she was crying too, all three of us just as loud as we could.

Annie stopped first and got up. She picked up Jimmy and took my hand, leading us over to the corner of that big downstairs room that served as a kitchen. She sat Jimmy down in a chair, and I sat down too. She stood there, glaring at us with those owlish eyes. Jimmy was so little his chin hardly came up to the tabletop, and he started to pull himself up. "Sit still!" Annie yelled in this terrible voice. Jimmy froze. I did too. "You almost died doing that, Jimmy!" she screamed at him. He looked puzzled. *"Be careful!"* she yelled at the top of her lungs, *"Both of you."* And then her anger was spent.

That night, when she took us home, she marched right up the steps to Mama and barged in on her. Jimmy and I stood at the bottom of the steps, and then he started up and I, naturally, followed him. I heard her tell Mama what had happened to Jimmy, and I could hear Mama's voice rise in concern.

"Is he all right? Where is he?"

"Stay put," Annie said. "He's fine. By the absolute grace of God. You've got to get up, Frances. I can't handle this, and Edda can't either. Besides, she's got to go back to school tomorrow."

"I know. I know. Are you sure he's all right?"

"He's all right. But I can't stand it, Frances. I don't know how you do it. I'm worn out."

Mama giggled. It was nice to hear it. Jimmy had crawled up to the top step and into her room in no time. I felt kind of shy about going in, but she called out to me. "Edda, are you out there? Come in here." She patted the bed beside her, and I sat down. She put her arm around me. She had Jimmy on the other side. "What happened? Are you okay?" She was asking me.

"I'm okay, Mama."

"Well, what happened?"

"I wasn't watching him is what happened. I'm sorry." I really was, and I started crying again thinking about it and how it would have been my fault if Jimmy had died.

"I know, baby, I know, sweetheart." She was crooning in her sweetest voice. "He's okay. It's what we call a cheap education. He won't go near a plug again until he's a grown man and finds out how much electricians cost."

I didn't understand what she was saying, but I knew she wasn't mad. Annie said, "Frances, you should have never let those two go to the funeral in the first place. I'm surprised at you. They're nothing but babies."

"I am not a baby," I answered her back. It shocked me to hear Annie refer to me that way.

"Well, you're too young for that kind of goings-on. You haven't been yourself since." She glanced at my mother. "She's been dreamy and brooding like I don't know what. Yes I do. Like her mother."

"Oh Annie, lay off," Mama said. "Edda, I wasn't sure if you should go the funeral or not. I hope it didn't do you any harm." Her voice was so kind.

"It didn't, Mama. I'm okay." I gave Annie a hard look.

"Well, I tried to think what was best to do. I couldn't talk to Ed about it, obviously." She gave a little laugh. "We never talked about such a thing. I have no idea what he would have preferred. It seems there was so much we didn't plan for. There's so much you never expect. I was doing the best—I—could. I don't know if it was right or not. I haven't planned for any of this." She sounded like she was going to cry. Her eyes were already leaking tears.

"Frances, I know that," Annie said softly. "We're all upset. I'm sorry." She included me in her look.

"Listen," I said, "all that happened was I got cold. At the funeral. I got cold. Okay? I'm glad I went, Mama. I mean it."

"Okay," she said and gave me a kiss. "This is just like Ed to die and not be here when I have to make an important decision like whether the kids should go to his funeral."

We were all silent for a moment, and then Mama and Annie both burst out giggling. They giggled for three or four minutes, getting more and more tickled as they'd catch each other's eye. "It's so inconsiderate," Mama said between giggles, and that started them off bigger than before.

That night Mama came into our room and tucked me in. She didn't sing like she used to. She didn't sing again for a long time, but she did come and sit and pat my hair and cheek. She did rock Jimmy till he went off, sucking on his fingers, and she was up the next morning, fixing breakfast. That's how it was we came to live without Daddy.

Chapter 5

Henry John Fitzpatrick came around again that next week. We were eating supper. He knocked on the back door, there where we were, in the kitchen. Most people came to the front. Mama's eyes got big and wide, sort of frightened looking when she saw who it was. She got up real slow and pulled open the door. There was a cold, rainy wind blowing that night; his face and hair were wet.

"Come in," Mama said. She looked over at Jimmy and me and then back up at him. Down at him maybe. One thing about Henry John I never could get straight was his size. Sometimes that man looked like a gnome and sometimes he looked big and tall and powerful. That night, if I recall, he was hunched up into himself. He looked every bit as scared as Mama.

"I didn't mean to interrupt your supper, Mrs. Combs. I can come back. Or I don't have to, if you'd rather I didn't." He was looking doubtful.

"No, no. Come in. Would you like a bite to eat?" Mama said. Then she did something: she switched her plate real fast from her seat to Daddy's and sat down in his chair. "Have a seat," she said to Henry John, indicating her own chair.

He sat down but shook his head about the bite to eat. "I brought some things of Ed's," he said. "They're out in the car. It's nothing much."

"Well, thank you, I'm sure," Mama said stiffly.

They were both of them sitting there, staring at each other as hard as I've ever seen people do it. I looked over at Jimmy, but he was just eating his meatloaf. With his fingers, of course. Mama had that look she'd had during those house days before the funeral. She was sitting up straight and taking him in with her eyes, bending her head forward a little to focus on him even more. I thought maybe this is who she'd been looking for. Now that I knew who he was. Henry John looked stricken, like a deer caught in car lights. He stared back and didn't move. I spilled my milk and broke the spell.

Somebody had to do it.

Everybody started at once. I said, "I'm sorry." Mama said, "Go get a washcloth and wring it out right now, quick." Henry John scooted back his chair real fast to avoid getting milk in his lap. Jimmy laughed and banged on his highchair tray: Good show. While I was cleaning up and Mama was saying, "Edda, don't just slop it around, mop it *up*," things got back to normal. Or as close to normal as things ever did get back to after Daddy died and Henry John came around.

"Would you like a cup of coffee?" Mama asked him. She was clearing up her plate and walking down to the sink.

"Well, if you're sure it's no trouble. Can I help?"

"Sit, sit," Mama scolded. "I've got it made. There's always coffee. Thank God, there's always coffee." They both laughed. "How do you take it?"

"Just a little milk." That's just how Daddy took it. She brought two cups over and took the dishrag out of my incompetent hands. "That's pretty good, Edda," she lied, finishing up the job in one cleansing sweep. Mama could make things clean just by looking at them. "You all finish up your supper, will you?" She looked mock-sternly at Jimmy, who was smearing mashed potatoes on his cheeks. He smiled at her sweet as could be. Henry John was just looking at us all with his sad, sad eyes.

"Mrs. Combs, uh, kids, I just want to say how terrible, how awful I feel about what happened. Oh God. I don't know what to say." His voice was husky and in some way sounded like Mama's.

Mama was staring into her cup and moving her lips around. She didn't say anything. I didn't either. Jimmy looked at Henry John and said, "Hi," bright as morning.

"Hi," Henry John replied out of reflex. I could tell he was surprised but pleased. He and Mama caught each other's eyes and smiled.

"Edda, can you get him started on his bath tonight?" Mama asked. I knew she was trying to get rid of us.

"Oh, Mama, can't we have dessert?" I begged. I was

stalling for time, and besides, she always gave us dessert. Mama once told me that she had grown up her whole childhood and never tasted dessert because her grandmother, who raised her, didn't believe in it. When she got grown and had kids of her own, she gave them dessert every night. It was chocolate pudding that night.

It used to be that when Mama made chocolate pudding, it would come out just right—four servings and four of us to eat it. Later, after Daddy had been dead a long time, she quit eating it altogether. She'd make four servings and it would last two days, two each for Jimmy and me. (Banker was never big on sweets.) That night she gave Henry John Daddy's portion. Course it wasn't Daddy's; he was dead before she ever made it. It was just an extra. But to me it felt like it was Daddy's. Or maybe I had planned to have it for myself. I was pretty sure Mama would've let me have it had I asked. Whatever the case, Henry John ate that bowl of pudding, and I got my nose out of joint because of it. The pudding was just the last straw. It was everything: knowing who he was now, and watching him and Mama look and look into each other's eyes.

When I did take Jimmy up to bathe, I was out of sorts with him. He was splashing in the tub and getting me wet. Then, when I was trying to put his diaper on and his pajamas, he was squirmy and hard to handle, and I yanked on his arm too hard and made him cry. I took him into Banker's room.

"He's impossible," I told Banker crossly, half shoving

Jimmy into the room. He went over to Banker and started chewing on his shoelace. "Hell and damnation," I said irritably.

"Now, Edda," Banker said mildly. He let me say about whatever I wanted to and never told on me, no matter what it was. "Where's Frances?"

"She's downstairs. With Mr. Henry John Fitzpatrick if you know who *he* is."

"No. Who is he? I don't believe I've made his acquaintance quite yet."

"Banker, don't you know?"

"No. Know what?"

"Well, Annie told *me*," I informed him self-importantly. "And *he* just as much said it himself downstairs. He's the man that blowed Daddy up. God, Banker. Don't they tell you anything?"

"Now, Edda."

"Jimmy, quit that," I snapped. He had almost all of Banker's shoe in his mouth now, chewing away. Banker was sitting in his chair with his legs crossed, paying him not the least bit of mind.

"Well, I don't think he's down there anymore, if that's any consolation to you, girl. I heard a car go off while you were bathing Jimmy. Come here, boy," he said, and Jimmy crawled up into his lap.

I walked over to his table and looked at his cuttings, picked up his magnifying glass, touched his scissors. I always liked looking at his stuff.

"I've got the clipping on your dad. Do you want to see it?" Banker asked.

"No," I said quickly and came away from his table like it had bit me. I hated that Daddy was in there somewhere, in the paper, in black and white. "Banker, I'm going downstairs."

"So I'm stuck with you," I heard him say to Jimmy in his most pleasant let's-play voice. I shut the door.

Mama was on the phone, and she waved me away when I came clattering down the steps. "Do you have any homework?" she whispered to me out of the side of her mouth. I shook my head no. Miss Jenkins believed in homework, but there were spells when we got away without it.

I made myself scarce around the corner and sat quietly on the couch in the living room.

"He came over here tonight is what I'm saying," Mama said. "Yes. Here." She waited a minute. "No, I don't know. He wanted to give me some money. What? . . . No, that's crazy, Annie. I don't think so. . . . He brought over some stuff of Ed's. I don't know, nothing much, his spare shirt and his jacket. He wasn't wearing his jacket, you know? . . . What? . . . Listen, I can barely hear you. . . . And some sheet music he said Ed loaned him. Now where in the world do you think Ed got sheet music is what I can't figure out. . . . What? . . . I don't know. Wait a minute, I'll get it." She put down the phone and came into the living room. "Edda, go to bed," she said to me. "I'll be up in a few minutes." I just stared at her. "Where's Jimmy?"

"Banker's got him," I said.

"Okay," she said, absent already, reaching into a pile on the chair that I hadn't noticed before. It startled me to realize that that was Daddy's jacket, a blue and white windbreaker. He was a Kentucky Wildcat fan, and those were their colors. Mama picked out a folder and went back to the phone. "Go to bed," she said once more, over her shoulder, to me. I never moved.

"Are you there? Annie? . . . Umm. Here it is, 'Brown Haired Becky.' Do you know it? . . . Yeah," she said after a long pause, and her voice was soft again. "He loved that song." She was quiet then for a long time except for little sounds in her throat that sounded like *mmm*. She made that sound a lot when people talked to her, nodding her head at them as if to encourage them to go on. I imagined her in there, sitting on the telephone stool, nodding her head at the phone.

I kept looking at Daddy's jacket, and finally I got up and touched it. Just a finger at first; then I picked it up. It was cold and sort of sweaty feeling. It smelled just like vinyl, not a bit like Daddy. In the pocket I found some coins—pennies and nickels and such. I held them in my hand. There was also a wrinkled-up chewing gum wrapper. My father never wadded up paper and threw it down; he was no litterbug. He always saved it for a proper garbage can and told me to do the same. (One day, when he was about three or four, Jimmy threw a soft drink cup out the window of the car. Mama and I were both stunned. She stopped the car, pulled off the road right there, and turned around to look at him. He didn't know it was wrong. That struck us both. He was innocent. "I guess we never taught him that yet, Edda," Mama said to me. So we taught him there, and I used Daddy's words, "Pick up your own mess." It was sharing something with Jimmy that belonged to him, and it felt good.)

Besides the jacket there was a calendar, the kind that hangs up on a wall. It had a picture of a mountain on it, but not the kind we had in Fincastle County. This one was huge, with snowcaps and hardly any trees on it.

I heard Mama laugh, and the sound of it was harsh and unexpected. I jumped and went back to the couch. "Annie," I heard her say, "you have the most suspicious mind I've ever encountered on a grown woman who wasn't already locked up. Now quit. No. No more. I'll see you tomorrow. No. I mean it. Good-bye." She didn't hang up though. I could tell she was still listening. "No," she said again, only this time very softly. "Annie, quit. Please. . . . What? Okay. Come for supper, why don't you. Bye." She hung up the phone. I could hear that she was limping before I ever saw her. She must have been tired.

"Edda, what is it, for heaven's sake? I told you to go to bed twenty minutes ago. Go." She made a sweeping motion toward the steps, but I didn't move.

"What's he want, Mama? That's what I want to know. What does Mr. Henry John Fitzpatrick want?" I was angry and feeling sassy. I don't think she noticed, or if she did, she let it go.

"He doesn't want anything, girl. You heard what he said."

"Do you know who he is? Banker didn't know. Do you?" She gave me a sideways look.

"If you mean do I know that he set the charge on the dynamite, yes. I've known it all along. He was at the hospital before I was, and he stayed almost as much. Does that answer your question, miss?"

I couldn't say a word. It seemed too much for her to be angry at me. And I knew she was. She never called me "miss" unless she was mad. Why wasn't she angry at *him*?

"Edda," she said, and this time her voice was lower and not so rough, "it's hard on him too. Try to understand that. Your daddy's dying was a mistake, a big, huge, horrible mistake. You can blame Mr. Fitzpatrick if you want, but it won't bring your daddy back. Nothing will. And the man's already blaming himself." Her eyes were tearing, and she rubbed them with the heel of her hand.

"Nobody gets out of here scot-free, Edda. Everybody hurts. It's part of the admission price as far as I can tell. But it's what we've got, child—life. We've still got it, and I know Ed wouldn't want you going around bitter and maybe even adding to someone else's pain by doing so. Do you understand that?"

"Yes. No. Do you?" My voice was barely a squeak. Mama pulled me to her and hugged me very hard.

"I understand that I love you," she said, leaking tears onto my neck.

We both heard Jimmy start to squall up in Banker's room. I could hear Banker, even from downstairs, saying, in what was still a pleasant voice, "Oh dammit to hell. What's the matter? Jimmy, come over here." Mama got up slowly, using me to push up on. As we climbed the steps, I noticed she was practically dragging her bad leg. She may have seen my glance or sensed my concern because she started quizzing me on spelling, which, besides telling time, was my worst subject and took my whole attention.

Chapter 6

My mother never intended to find herself a widow, with two children and an old man to care for, at the age of twenty-eight. But she was. And I know she never meant to end up on Cauley's Creek, which is way far up and gone in the southeastern tip of Kentucky. She was from Pittsburgh, Pennsylvania, and had hoped for better things. So she said.

It's hard to know much about her childhood; she shut the door on it a long time ago and never opened it. At least not to me, and I asked. Her own parents, who were from Alabama or Louisiana, someplace like that, had died or gone off, one when she was very small. Her grandparents, whom I never met, raised her in Pittsburgh until she was fifteen. At which point she ran away. From fifteen on she'd tell about herself, but before that, forget it. She'd just pick out the nearest corner or cloud to stare at and shake her head.

I do know how she and Daddy met. I've heard that tale a thousand times. It was at a McDonald's in New York City. He was fresh out of the army; she was eighteen and working her way around the northeast, taking it in. Mama was there handing out hamburgers, literally. (She was fired from that McDonald's for giving away food. She'd been doing it all along, but the night they met was the night she actually lost her job for it.) Mama was a soft touch for anybody who looked the least bit hungry, and she was known among the street people (or whatever they called them back then) in that section of the city. Daddy'd been sitting there, eating his food and watching her. He'd seen the manager watching her as well, which she had not. Daddy'd seen him walk over to her, seen her look up in surprise. He'd seen the manager take her away and seen her come out, ten minutes later, dressed in street clothes and looking pitiful.

Daddy picked her up is what he did, bought her a cup of coffee at a little place down the street. They used to say they were going back there someday, when they could get a vacation. Basically, what happened—without going into too much detail, which I'm certain neither one of them would appreciate—what happened was they fell in love. Daddy was headed back to Kentucky in a few days, and he took her with him. He still had a year or two to finish in college; he was a forestry major. Later he took some engineering. He was trying to reclaim strip mines, which was how he came to be up there on Rattlesnake Mountain where he got blown up. Mama decided to see if she couldn't go back to school too. They came to Lexington, Kentucky, and signed on at the university. Mama took a job at a Burger King there (fast food was her specialty) and got her high school diploma. Once she set her mind to studying, she found out she was good at it, and in no time she had herself a scholarship.

After two years they were married, and exactly one year later, on their anniversary, they had me. I was born in Lexington, at the Baptist hospital. When I was almost two years old, we moved up to Cauley's Creek, where Daddy had a job with the state, inspecting strip mines. Mama had her college degree by then, in history. She too had a job, working at home writing lesson plans for a high school history book. One of my earliest memories is coming across my mother sitting on the living room floor with papers and books and maps spread all around her, like a giant skirt, a vast distance of paper across which I had to wade to get to her.

Banker came to live with us then too; he was some kind of kin to Daddy. Neither one of them got along too well with the rest of the family, but they got along great with each other, and Banker needed a place to stay that winter. When Daddy died, I know there was some question raised about his leaving; Banker brought it up himself. He asked Mama one evening, when we'd brought him up his supper, if she thought maybe it was time for him to move on. She cried out loud, put his tray down, and sat in his lap like she was a kid, with her arms flung up around his neck. "Banker, I need you," she cried. "Please don't go." And he never did, until he died last year.

Mama had finished up her textbook work by the time

Jimmy was born, and she didn't have a job of any kind when Daddy was killed. For that whole first year she didn't work; she told me we lived on insurance money and social security checks. In the spring she started talking about how pretty soon she was going to have to get a job, and how I'd have to help out more.

Looking back on it, it seems strange to me that we stayed on Cauley's Creek as long as we did. We didn't have any real people up there to speak of, besides ourselves. And having people is one of the very main things about living there. I'd often felt out of place at school when teachers or other kids would try to place me. They'd say, "Now, whose girl are you?" and I'd say, "Frances and Ed Combs'," and they'd say, "Are they any kin to the Second Creek Combses?" and I'd say, "No, my people are from over by Pikeville." Pikeville, although it's also in eastern Kentucky, seemed, and was, a long way from Spence. And certainly Mama's people, whoever they might be, dead or alive in Pittsburgh, were no help at all. After Daddy died, I got a little more respect at school. My father being dead at an early age was enough to gain me a certain amount of notoriety and acceptance. Which I enjoyed.

There were no fast food places in Spence where Mama could work, and I guess nobody was writing textbooks just then either. I remember her going into Banker's room and talking to him about it. We all took our problems to Banker. And he never solved them. But he listened. He could really listen.

"Banker, I don't know what I'm fit to do anymore."

"Now, Frances, you're a young woman," he said. I never thought of her like that when I was a kid, but she *was* young, relatively.

"Well, I feel old, Banker, as old as these hills. Which might be why I'm still here. I identify with them. I sure don't know what's going to become of us if we stay on, but I don't think I can work up the energy to move, just now. I don't know. . . ." She was leaking tears.

"How bad is the money, Frances?" Banker asked. "Perhaps, I could draw a little more, or get food stamps or somesuch to help out."

"No, I don't want you doing that. The money's not critical quite yet, but it's not going to be enough to support us forever. Sooner or later I'm going to have to get a job."

"Oh yes, I read about this all the time." Banker nodded his head. "Working mothers."

Mama chuckled. "It's newsworthy, is it? Oh boy. Banker," she said in a serious tone, "tell me—what do you think I'm good at? Edda, you too. Think. What can I do?"

"Well"—Banker considered—"your cooking's tolerable."

"Sweet of you to say so, Mr. Combs," she said in a voice not quite her own, "especially since I have reason to believe you know better, being a man of such wide experience and all." She gave him a funny face. "But if you think for one minute I'm going to spend my time standing on my feet in a hot kitchen any more than I have to to keep the bunch of you fed, you are sadly misinformed as to my character."

This way of talking was a little joke between her and Banker, dating back to when they first met and he'd called her "highfalutin." Sometimes she'd spin sentences out by the yard. Banker loved it, and Jimmy and I did too because it meant she was in a good mood. And Mama's good moods were like candy to us all. For so many months that first winter after Daddy died, she barely spoke, and never more than she had to—never talking for the pure pleasure of the words and the happy thing you could sense they were leading to. Once she felt better, she went back to telling Jimmy and me bedtime stories, singing to us too, after a long time of not. She believed that stories should have happy endings; that's the only kind she'd tell. She was that way about movies too.

Mama said, "Forget cooking. I don't like standing up all day anyway. I don't think my leg can take it."

"Well . . ." Banker scratched his chin and thought. I did too.

"You can read," I volunteered. She was always reading books.

"That's a good point, Edda, thank you. I can read. What else?"

"You can sing, Frances, I think you sing real pretty," Banker said.

"Well, thank you, Banker," Mama said with her head tucked down. She was embarrassed, I could tell. She sighed. "Surely something will come up. I keep thinking I could do a good job taking care of people, like a nurse or something. But I just can't see going back to school again right now."

"You'd make a fine nurse, Frances, I'm sure of it."

"Oh, Mama, no," I blurted out. The idea of her being up at the hospital (which was the only place I'd ever seen nurses) seemed awful to me. It seemed to be tempting fate for her to get a job there, the place Daddy had disappeared from.

"Well, let's not worry about it until we have to," she said, giving me her long look, black eyes narrowed down to a slit.

Later I heard her talking to Annie about the same subject. Annie was telling her to get away. "You got the whole world open to you, Frances; you're a young woman. Don't bury yourself up here on Cauley's Creek."

"Sounds close to what I told *you* when Irv left." Mama smiled.

"Well, it is. And I might leave, as you know, when I finish."

Annie was painting portraits of people who lived up and down that holler. Later they would be published in a book called *Up on Cauley's Creek* that became mildly famous for a short time. She wouldn't paint Jimmy or me because we weren't pureblood, and Annie was very big on authenticity.

"Well, the point I want to run home to you, Fran, is to do *something*," Annie continued. "You're going to waste away up here."

"I'll do something, I'll do something for sure, don't worry. I just can't seem to wake up enough to do anything about it right now. I'm okay. Just tired."

This was the truth. Mama slept a lot that first year. I'd find her on the couch or in her bed when I came home from school. She even fell asleep at the table one day after dinner.

She said, "You know, I've figured something out about myself lately. It used to be I was all the time getting upset and emotional about these little things. Anything. I let it throw me. Ed was so down-to-earth I could afford to get absolutely flighty about whatever I wanted. It was a luxury in a way. What I was doing, and I didn't realize it till just recently, was sort of holding God off."

"What do you mean?" Annie laughed short and loud. "If you're going to go get born again on us, Frances, I quit. I mean it."

"Oh, Annie." Mama smiled at her friend and reached over to her. She was patting Annie's hand the way she would with me or Jimmy when we were upset. "Listen, okay? Just listen. What I was doing, and I didn't even know it, was saying, 'Look God, I'm already upset. Don't throw anything more my way. I'll take the little things to heart, and you won't have to teach me by knockout, by taking it to extremes. I'll get the point early. Let my children be okay; don't give me cancer; don't let my husband die.' " She broke off and shook her head. "Can you understand this?" She wiped away the tears that had begun to stream down her cheeks as she talked.

"I think I do," Annie said.

"Well, now I've found out my deal didn't work. God didn't play along, or I had the rules all wrong. I don't know what happened except that Ed is gone. God threw me one of the big ones anyway. Unsolicited, you might say. So I've started to reconsider. If getting upset about the little things doesn't help ward off the big ones, then why do it? I'm not saying I intend to become calm and rational or anything drastic, but maybe a little. Annie, this is still kind of new inside. Do you understand what I'm saying?"

"I do, Frances, I really do. And I'm glad you're feeling that way."

I don't know if Mama ever really did stop fretting the small stuff. It seemed to me she was always watching us children awfully close, whether we needed it or not. And she cried for the rest of her life at a full moon—things like that. But I know she tried to take on some of Daddy's levelheadedness. At first it was an act of will, a way of keeping close to him. Eventually, I suspect, it came home to her that, like it or not, she was in charge. We depended on her and did what she said. Once a teacher of mine referred to her as a "sensible woman," which she was not, but I can understand how someone who knew her only slightly might think so.

Chapter 7

It was March of the following year that Mama first started working. I was in the fourth grade, and Jimmy was almost three years old. It had been a hard, cold winter. That spring the icy slush in the creek behind our house ran longer and higher than ever before. We'd been snowed in for much of January and February; I'd missed at least a month of school. Long after the main roads are clear down there, the hollers stay treacherous. There were families that lived further out on Cauley's Creek, and elsewhere, that didn't get out until April that year. But then, lots of them only came out once a month anyway to go to town and get their groceries, maybe a check.

Annie drove a Jeep, and she made sure of us every few days, even during the worst of it. She always brought food and some disposable diapers for Jimmy. Mama said Daddy wouldn't have approved of us using them, their being plastic and all, but we used them anyway. After the lines in the house froze up, they burst, and what water we used we had to carry. Lots of days we were cold. Mama and Jimmy and

I would sit around the coal stove in the living room. She let us watch a lot of TV that winter. Banker stayed up in his room, fortified by an electric heater. He said he was fine.

Henry John came around several times that winter. He'd given us presents at Christmas: stilts for me, a record for Mama of Beethoven's Ninth Symphony, I forget what for Jimmy, and a subscription for Banker to the Sunday *New York Times*. It got to our house on Tuesday or Wednesday every week, and Banker would actually rub his hands together in delighted anticipation when I'd bring it up to him.

In March Henry John told Mama about a job of secretary at the coal company where he worked. His head was under the sink; he was fixing the pipes. "I don't know if you'd want it or not, Frances, but I'll check on it for you. Gladly." This last word rang out louder than the rest, perhaps he raised his head to make sure it got out from under the sink. Gladly.

"Secretary, you say." She was sitting on the floor in the corner with her knees up and her skirt drawn under her. "I expect I could do that. I might as well. I'm going to have to do something to bring in some—" She paused, cut off her words, and glanced sharply at Jimmy and me, who were also on the floor, listening and watching the spectacle of Henry John fixing the pipes. "—income," she finished carefully.

Henry John's blue-jeaned legs and hips would wriggle

and bend. Jimmy was dodging the heavy work boots that would kick around wildly at unpredictable intervals. Every now and then Henry John's hand and hairy arm would reach out and grab a tool, or Mama would hand him one. Besides his conversation with Mama he kept up a constant mutter about the pipes. "Dammit all," he would say occasionally, the words thumping out from underneath the cabinet. I'd giggle. "Dammit all," Jimmy would echo like it was music, and Mama would shake her head no at him but smiling herself.

When he finally came out completely, his face was streaked with sweat and oil. "These are worse than the ones in the bathroom. They may go out again on you, I can't say for sure."

"Well, I thank you kindly for what you've done, Henry John," Mama said in the formal way she addressed him back then. She was getting to her feet. "How about some coffee?"

"Oh, yes. There's always coffee." Henry John said it slowly, as though just then finding those words of hers in his memory and repeating them carefully. I may be wrong. It could be that he had said those words to himself all winter and the year before too, that he remembered things about her just before he went to sleep, the way people do when they're in love. But it sounded as though the words were new to him, as he might speak them in French or some other foreign language he was just learning.

Years later he told me he had been in love with Mama

from the moment he saw her, flying into the emergency room at the hospital that first day when Daddy got blown up. Blown up by him. By mistake. How horrible for him to fall in love just then. With her. But that's how he remembers it, or so he says. From that moment. And he never said horrible; that's my word.

That day in the kitchen, when he sat there drinking coffee and telling her about the job, he was in love. I was old enough, at ten, to suspicion it but not to call it by name. Mama may have known, but I don't think she did; she never acted like it anyway. Not then. She was still turned in on herself, on us, on her memories. I don't think she had room to love yet, or energy even to notice it. She was kind to Henry John, perhaps because he was clearly in pain, and it was her way to be gentle with hurting things. The sadness never left his eyes; they were much like her own. Love, loss. Not quite the same, but close.

She was smoking a cigarette, a habit she took up after Daddy died. "I do know how to type," she said, blowing out smoke in a sigh. "I learned when I was in the eighth grade, and I'm not bad, I don't think."

"I'm sure you can do it, Frances. I'll call about it tonight if you like. I don't mind calling Robby at home." Robby was Mr. Robinson's nickname. He ran the company or owned it or both. At any rate, he was Henry John's boss, the man who became Mama's boss.

"I have to think about what to do with Jimmy," she said, glancing at me, considering. "And Edda too, for that matter," she concluded. I smiled at her, happy for once to have been found lacking.

Jimmy was a job. I watched him plenty and I know. That day, he and I went out and stood by the rushing creek. We were both fascinated by the icy white-capped water, but being older I had more fear of it. Jimmy raced up to the bank and acted like he was going to jump in. I grabbed the back of his jacket and told him no, it was dangerous. At three he was old enough to mind, and he did, pretty much. But he was the kind of kid you couldn't turn your back on for a minute for fear of what he'd get into next. He looked at that water with longing. It was cold still, although crocuses were out. That bank was pretty, not stunning like Heaven—which I couldn't even get to that year until May because of high water—but brown and gold and green with fallen leaves and new growth coming through. Mrs. Roosevelt was there too, sitting back from the bank considerably, in a patch of sun, calmly looking, as cats do.

After a while, Henry John and Mama came out too. He was ready to go, but they too watched the water. "It's high," he said.

"The man at the store said it was the highest since 1937," Mama said. "I suppose you heard about the flooding in Hazard?"

"Yes. Matter of fact, a couple of us went down to help the Army Corps of Engineers. There was considerable damage."

"Oh." Mama turned and looked at him. "You know, Ed said this would happen."

Henry John looked startled. "What would?"

"The flooding. He predicted it would only get worse as long as they were strip-mining up here."

I thought about my father predicting things. Had he not died, it wouldn't have been a prediction; it would have been something else—an opinion he held or something he said. He would have been standing there with us, saying it. Or would he? We'd grown used to using the past tense about him. That he could predict seemed to put him in the future as well.

"He was right, I suppose," Henry John said. "I don't care for it myself, but it's a living." Mama nodded and looked away, back at the water.

"I don't know what he would think of me going to work for them—a coal company, I mean."

"I don't either, Frances. But he was the only inspector the guys on the crew ever liked. And I think he liked us. He acted like he did."

This was the most I had ever heard Henry John say about my daddy up till then. And I already knew he was liked; people were always telling me that.

"Inspecting strip mines for the government is a risky business in this part of the country, and even more so if you're not corrupt, which Ed was not," Mama said. She was referring to a friend of Daddy's, also uncorrupt, who'd just been shot at over in Knott County. Such things happened fairly regularly to the state inspectors. He and his wife had been over for dinner the week before. His arm was still in a sling from where the bullet had nipped him. They were moving out of state. Both Mama and Henry John fell silent, remembering perhaps, as I was, that Daddy didn't die from gunfire.

"Do you feel out of place here, not being local?" Henry John asked her, shifting the subject. He too was from someplace else, from Pittsburgh in fact. It was one of those things, a coincidence. Although they never met back there, they grew up within ten blocks of each other. There were a number of such links between them.

"Oh yes, of course. But I feel out of place everywhere, so I'm not certain it counts," Mama said.

"Well, I do," he said. "I don't think I could ever get used to it up here. I'm not sure I would want to. But Ed, being local, it made a difference with him. The guys respected him."

"He wasn't local to here," I said. This seemed important to me, having suffered from it at school. "He was from Pikeville." Both grown-ups smiled at me, indulgently. I hated that. "Well, he wasn't," I added, as if that settled it.

"No. You're right; he wasn't local from here," Mama agreed. "But he means local from this part of the"—she waved her arms at the creek, the trees—"world. You know what he means, Edda."

"What I meant," Henry John said quickly, "is that he

understood people here, and respected them. That's what I meant. And that they respected him too. He got more strip-mine law enforced around here than any other inspector I've ever known or heard of."

Mama sighed and nodded her head in agreement. "He had a way about him," she said in her dreamy, far-off voice.

"Yes, he did," Henry John answered like an amen.

Chapter 8

So Mama started work. After school, instead of going home on the bus, I'd go over to Mrs. Stumbo's. She lived in town and kept kids. She kept Jimmy all day and me after school and in the summer. Mrs. Stumbo was short and blond and wore a lot of makeup. When she was a high school senior, about twenty years before, she'd been elected Miss Upper Kentucky River, a beauty queen. She told me how she had ridden on a float with ribbons on it, over in Barbourville. They'd put Vaseline on her teeth so they wouldn't dry out from smiling all day. She liked to talk about it and talk to me about my looks. Sometimes she cut my hair, but it never did much good.

Besides us, she kept several other children: Janie and Joanie Piper, who were twin five-year-olds, and Bobby McIntosh, a little baby. Her husband was a lawyer in Spence, and they lived in a big brick home. For some reason, if it's brick, people call it a home, especially in town; if it's flat white plank wood, like ours was, and up some holler like Cauley's Creek, it's a house; if it's even farther up the creek and peeling or made of logs, like Annie's, it's a cabin or maybe a shack. Mrs. Stumbo opened her home to children because she just *loved* children, or so she told Mama. They didn't have any children of their own. Yet. That's how she always said it—yet.

I was the oldest child there until summer, when Bill Peyton and Amy Eversole joined us; both of them were in the same grade with me in school. None of us liked it much. It was boring, and we were embarrassed about being baby-sat. Sometimes Mama would let me stay home with Banker or go down to Annie's, but not often. Mostly, Amy and I hung around in the yard, climbed trees, and snuck up onto the garage roof, from which we jumped. It was high enough to constitute daring but low enough that we rarely did more than numb our knees and shins when we landed. Mr. Stumbo saw us at it one day and said it was off limits, at which point it became a double dare.

That summer Amy taught me to ride a bike. In town there were sidewalks and a few flat places where I could pick up speed enough to get the knack of balancing. I wasn't very good at it and got much more bruised from that bicycle than I ever did from the garage roof.

Mrs. Stumbo had a fenced-in yard for the little ones. I asked Jimmy one time if he remembered her, and he said all he could recall was the fence. Most of the day he sat out there with a spoon, digging in a corner of the yard. I think he was trying to escape. He cried a lot when Mama started taking him there. Even in the summer, when I joined him, he was still crying when she left. Mama cried too, only in *her* way, silently, tears slipping out of her eyes when she'd turn to wave at us, walking away in her clicking heels.

At home Mama would tell us funny stories about Mr. Robinson, whom she made out to be a clown, fat and puffing. I never met the man, but I can't believe he was as ridiculous as she portrayed him to be. That was for our fun, to make us laugh. According to Mama, he did twenty-five things at once, each badly. He'd be drinking a cup of coffee, stirring it without watching, spilling coffee on papers he was supposed to be reading, when the phone would ring and he'd say in a deep, breathless voice that Mama would imitate, "I'll get it, I'll get it, Mrs. Combs, just you relax"; and he'd tangle up the cord swiveling around in his big chair, talking, drinking, stirring, shuffling papers, lighting a cigarette, searching for an ashtray. Someone would come in or the other phone would ring, and he'd try to do it all but would end up inevitably asking Mama in a whisper, "Now who am I talking to?" Or even funnier, the way she told it, "What am I doing?"

She wouldn't stop till we laughed. She'd go on making the scene more and more absurd until I'd say, half giggling, half taken in, "Really?" And she'd nod then, and knowing she almost had us, she'd elaborate some more until Jimmy and I would burst out laughing at the physical slapstick of it all. She needed us to laugh. I could feel it. To this day I can't stand comedy routines; the responsibility is too much for me. The man or woman stands on the stage needing the audience to laugh. If they don't, they make jokes about that, but I can feel the real tension rising. It almost makes me sick. I get panicky and laugh too much.

Being funny, making us laugh, was Mama's way of taking care of us, of reassuring herself that we were okay, that she was doing a good job. If we were laughing, surely she was a good mother. Jimmy had started having night terrors. He'd wake up screaming in the night and scream on and on, even after he was awake, or appeared to be. Neither Mama nor Banker nor I could calm him, and it was pitiful to see his fear, so raw, so close, night after night. Mama was sure it had something to do with her going to work. It probably did since that's exactly when the terrors started.

"But what can I do?" she'd ask Banker, ask me, ask Annie and anyone else she discussed it with. "What can I do?"

Our doctor, Dr. Napier, told her this was normal in some children at Jimmy's age, whether or not their mothers worked. He said it was nothing to worry about, to bring Jimmy out of it slowly, to turn on soft lights, talk quietly to him, maybe give him some water. All of which we did, night after night, while he sobbed and shuddered in fear of we still don't know what. He could not tell us what was wrong; even calming down, no words would come. He would choke on them, as if to utter them ensured worse to come.

In the morning he was the same as always. He woke up cheerful, ready to play and talk and hug. Only when Mama left Mrs. Stumbo's would he cry, pull on her skirt, and follow her to the door weeping, "Don't go, Mama, don't go." We'd watch her from Mrs. Stumbo's big picture window, see her wave and watch her get into the car, wiping her eyes. I'd hold Jimmy and talk to him, tell him, "Now, now, you know she's coming back. She's coming back." After a while he'd go into the yard and sit by the fence with his spoon.

So Mama wanted us to laugh, and laugh we did, almost every night at supper. The fun she made of Mr. Robinson was not unkind. She made fun of herself too in this same way, exaggerating little things until they assumed hysterical proportions. But one thing she never did, never, was make fun of us.

I was just then coming to an age where I took an interest in other people's families. Amy Eversole and I became best friends. I ate dinner at the Eversoles several times and discovered a number of things. One, other people's mothers don't tell funny stories every night, maybe never. Two, some people's mothers (and fathers too) make fun of them a *lot*. Amy's did. Amy had a goofy big laugh that I never noticed much at all until the night at her house when her mother said—at the table this was—said dry as dust, "Yuk, yuk, Amy, you sound like a chicken with a stone in its throat." Amy stopped laughing mid-yuk and turned pale, then red. I felt frightened. This was her mother, but it didn't sound right. It didn't sound like my mother, and it wasn't any fun.

Amy's father was a mild, colorless man who worked at

the bank. We only saw him now and then. But he too was capable of teasing in some odd way I was formerly unfamiliar with, past the point of fun, teasing till it hurt. One time, and it's remarkable that Amy and I stayed friends after this, I spent the night and wet the bed. I was ten years old, and there I was, wetting the bed. At a friend's house yet. Worst of all, we were sleeping together in a double bed. I awoke just after I did it, horrified, humiliated, resigned to anything. Amy slept on and in the morning said nothing at all. A few days later her father called me Edda Wetta as she and I passed through their living room, where he was sitting. Amy pulled me out into the hall and punched me in the stomach—to take my mind off it, I think. She and I liked to wrestle and sometimes gave each other stomach punches to tighten our muscles. We also did sit-ups and stretches. I'm trying to explain that her punching me in the stomach was her way of apologizing for her father.

And three, it was okay in their family to say "shut up," right to someone's face, okay for Amy and her older sister Andrea to yell at each other and say, "I hate you" and "Mom, I can't believe you had her." Andrea called Amy a failure of the pill one time. This was in the kitchen with Mrs. Eversole standing there. I didn't know what she was talking about, didn't know what "the pill" was, but knew certainly it was wrong for them to be yelling at each other. I thought Mrs. Eversole was going to do something—hit somebody or pound on the table and tell them to stop—but she only said, "So what, Andy. You were a failure of the diaphragm." To which Andy made a face and left the room.

Later Andrea explained to us as best she understood it what the pill and the diaphragm were. She told us too, when we asked, about periods and babies. I'd heard some of it before, but she made it sound interesting, dangerous. At fourteen she had a flair for the dramatic and the self-proclaimed desire to see Amy and me suffer. "Just wait," she'd say, smirking at us, carefully applying a smear of lipstick, smacking at herself in the mirror. "You'll get the curse early, Amy, I can tell. Look at those boobs already. And it's going to hurt, kid; you're going to wish you had never been born."

Maybe this sounds strange, maybe not, but I never thought about hurting Jimmy the way they hurt each other every day. He never thought like that about me either, I'm fairly positive. We didn't hate each other. I don't think Amy and Andrea hated each other either, not really. But they talked like they did, and no one ever told them not to.

So I learned some things over there and at Mrs. Stumbo's too. Amy had a crush on Bill Peyton, but I don't know why. For one thing he hated girls and us girls in particular, or so he said all the time. He sat in one chair in one room at Mrs. Stumbo's all day long, either reading his comic books (he had stacks) or watching TV. He had freckles and carroty red hair. He would turn bright red if he was angry or embarrassed, which was often if Amy and I were in the room. Sometimes he listened to ball games on the radio while he sat there reading his comics. Amy thought he was cute. She also thought he thought *she* was cute but was too shy to admit it. Something like that. I thought he was a snob. But talking about it with her made me feel excited.

At ten and eleven, we knew we were going to "grow up" as Andrea had threatened. We didn't know what all it would entail, or when exactly it would happen, but we were strong and thought we were ready for it. Between us, we thought we were ready for anything.

What I wasn't ready for was for Henry John to start courting Mama, out front. And more precisely, I wasn't ready for her to start going all gooey in return. They made me sick. I liked Henry John all right, I thought of him vaguely as some kind of relation, like Banker or Annie. I knew Annie wasn't really my aunt, but I thought of her that way; we all did—Mama's sister. And Henry John fit in there somewhere too. I'd quit thinking of him as the man who killed Daddy and considered him an uncle of sorts, maybe not even that. Just someone we knew who was nice or at least okay. But then it came out.

It started that summer when the evenings were long. Mama would have him over to supper, Annie too. She told me later she was thinking to fix them up, at least give them a chance to get to know one another.

Henry John played the guitar. He played it well—beautifully is not too much to say. After supper we would sit on the front porch, and he would pull it out and play. He and Mama, and Annie too sometimes, and sometimes Jimmy and I would sing along. It was fun. There was something in his music that was reassuring, like a blanket he pulled over our shoulders to keep us from the chill. Our voices sounded fine mingled in the night air, and the stars twinkled their approval on us all. Even Banker was found one night to have his door open and his foot tapping. Mama invited him down, and to everyone's astonishment, perhaps including his own, he came.

That night Banker sat on the porch rocker and belted out, in a voice I had never suspected was in him, tune after tune from what he called the olden days. Some part of Banker's olden days had been spent organizing men for the United Mine Workers. He was amazed and deeply pleased to find in Henry John a person who still knew the music. What Henry John didn't know, Banker would sing alone, a raspy, thick, strong voice booming out verse after verse. He knew all the words. "Dreadful Memories" he sang and "Colman's Mines," "Which Side Are You On, Boys?" and "Dark as a Dungeon," many more. We stayed up late that night, letting Banker lead us on.

But that was the only night he came down. Mostly Henry John played songs that came from the sixties, songs he and Mama and Annie, if she'd sing, knew. From listening to them I found out songs my father loved—old Beatles' stuff particularly.

Henry John, I believe, knew them all. Sometimes—no, often, in fact—Mama would begin weeping, leaking tears and brushing them away. "It's something music does to me," she'd explain. Not that Annie or Jimmy or I needed an explanation. We were used to it by then. It was just the way she was, not sad in any overwhelming sense of the word, just weeping. It was as though she had to keep a sense of proportion about all things and the balance of it came up tears.

The first night he played and she cried Henry John put down his guitar and wouldn't pick it up. He looked worried and sheepish, as if he had caused this, which in fact he had but not by his music. Mama was laughing and shaking her head, tears still streaming, saying, "Oh, Henry John, you mustn't pay it any mind. I'm fine. I thought you knew. Please don't stop. It was beautiful. I mean that. I don't want you to stop. Tell him, Edda—somebody."

"She does this all the time, Henry John, it's true," I volunteered.

"Edda's right," Annie backed me up. "Play."

He still looked doubtful, cast eyes all night at Mama, who would smile at him encouragingly. "It's nothing," she told him again as he was climbing into his truck. Jimmy and I were fooling around in the back of it. "It's something I do," she said. "I don't know. I seem to be especially susceptible to music."

"Well, maybe we shouldn't be rubbing salt in the wound, so to speak," he offered.

"Oh, no, I think there's no harm in tears. They just need to come out. It may be even that I'm crying over more than Ed, although that's when it started." She tilted her head away from him, looked down at some dark thing I could not make out, following her gaze. Henry John looked up at the sky. "I never cried much as a child," Mama said. "I think it's catching up with me is all. Your music made me happy tonight, Henry, not sad."

"It did? Are you sure?"

"Yes. It really did, and I thank you for it. Let's do it again sometime."

He drove off that night like he'd been summoned by the moon. His face was shining.

Chapter 9

My first real inkling of what was *really* going on came from Annie. Jimmy and I were down at her house picking raspberries on the hill. "Watch out for snakes," Annie would holler at us from the kitchen window every fifteen minutes or so—as if I wasn't already doing just that. Everybody knows snakes like a berry patch, although just why this is I don't know. Jimmy and I had carried Mrs. Roosevelt down with us for this very purpose. She wasn't much protection; mostly she stretched out in the sun and slept, but we both liked to think of her as a good snake cat.

Jimmy proceeded to eat his weight in berries, which was no small accomplishment. I was more interested in having something to show for my work and plonked away steadily, getting my ankles fairly cut up in the process. After a couple of hours we both got hot and called it quits. I had over three quarts, which is not a bad show for such a scraggly patch as what Annie had.

She was on the phone when we came in the house and waved us over to the sink, where I washed some of the purple off of Jimmy. When she hung up, she admired our load and poured us both some iced sugar tea.

"Well, it looks like I might finally get myself a carpenter to finish up this place," she said. Over the years Annie hired and quickly fired any number of workmen for all sorts of reasons. Her house was still much the same as Irv had left it: wires, wood, saws, and screwdrivers.

"Do you think we have enough to make jam?" I asked. She looked puzzled. I was thinking berries; she was thinking carpenters.

"Jam? Oh yeah. I'm sure you do. Is that what you intend to do with them?"

"Some," I said. "And some will just be fine the way they are over ice cream and whatnot." I smiled at her, hoping she might take the hint. She smiled back but made no move. "But Banker said something this morning about how he hankered after fresh raspberry jam, and you know, I thought . . ."

"Sure, we have enough to make Banker some jam. And if I'm not mistaken, there's another man hanging around over there who would probably like some too."

"Who?" I asked. I was startled to think of "another man" at our house.

"Why, Mr. Henry John Fitzpatrick is who. Isn't he still over there mooning around your mother? Crooning away?"

"Henry John?"

Annie just nodded, fixing me in the sights of her level gray-eyed gaze.

"Yeah," I said. "He's over there right now I think. He's patching a leak in the roof. But he never said anything about jam, Annie. What do you mean?"

"He's sweet on somebody over there. Come on, Edda, do you mean to tell me you never noticed? How old are you anyway?"

Had I noticed? I'd noticed Henry John looking at Mama; you couldn't help but notice that. His eyes were so big, so brown, so sad. But more than that? Something in the pit of my stomach knew, must have known all along without naming it. I looked at Annie. She shrugged.

"People will talk, that's what I'm worried about."

"Talk about what?" I asked. It was hard to follow all these lightning bolts; she tossed them at me as though they were berries. "Talk about what?" I asked again, for now she was only smiling at me, a tight curve on her lips.

"Think for a minute, Edda." Her tone was deep with disappointment that I should be so slow. I thought.

"You mean because they're both from Pittsburgh?" I asked at last. Perhaps that was something to talk about.

Annie rolled her eyes in exasperation. "Now there's a new angle I never considered," she said sarcastically.

"Annie, please." The game she was playing with me hurt my pride, but I was also frightened. There was menace in her tone, her hints. "What? I don't know, okay? What?"

Just that year at Spence Elementary the new gym had been finished and was consecrated (or however you break in gyms) with a little ceremony that the whole school attended. When it was over, we were allowed to walk around and look at the new equipment. In the middle of the still polished floor, painted on in a big red circle with yellow lettering, was a huge *S*. I innocently, stupidly asked the gym teacher what it stood for. Like a good teacher, like Annie, she made me figure it out for myself. Which I couldn't do. Super? I kept guessing. Superb? Supreme? Anxiety was making me blank. Serendipity? I guessed at last, knowing it couldn't be that but using the fine word I had just learned the week before as a balm for my overwhelming ignorance in things obvious. Mrs. Smith had looked at me with the same blend of humor and dismay that Annie was using. "Spence," she said at last, and I had flooded with shame. Of course. Anyone would know that.

"Edda," Annie said, and I could tell from her tone that, like Mrs. Smith, she had taken pity on this poor stupid child, "people will say it doesn't look right. If she takes up with him, I mean. After all, even though your father's— death—was an accident, of course it was, he *did* have something to do with it. Jimmy, get out of there," she yelled suddenly. "Out, out, out of there, now out on the porch with you. Now." This flurry of words aimed at Jimmy was perhaps designed to let me sit undisturbed while the meaning of the previous words, aimed at me, exploded inside me. People say, "It finally sunk in." This was not a sinking but a detonation. I could feel my ears ringing with the shattering of glass, metal, old beliefs.

By the time Annie had chased Jimmy out on the porch

and come back in, I had blown apart and reassembled in a form closely resembling my old self.

"What do *you* think?" I asked her, sipping my iced tea. It should have been whiskey, or coffee at least. I was as old as a ten-year-old can get.

But Annie was finished. "Oh, I don't know. I just want what's best for Frances and you all," she said.

We didn't talk about it again that day; instead we made jam. I moved around her kitchen with a new feeling— fragility. Coming back together, the pieces had not yet settled in place. I felt as though I might chip.

Late that afternoon Jimmy and Mrs. Roosevelt and I made our way back up the creek. We passed the familiar yards of our neighbors, saw the rusting cars parked here and there, the laundry hanging out, the big boys up at the Collier house playing dirt-lot basketball and drinking beer. Are these the people that will talk? I wondered. It seemed to me from my new eyes, my newly old self, that they were talking already. I took Jimmy's hand.

Sure enough, Henry John was still up at the house. Mama was fixing dinner, and he was standing in the kitchen, over by the sink, in her way, watching her. And talking. I could hear them talking before we even came up the back steps. Mama was laughing. That laugh gave me a sharp pain. It was a sound we hadn't heard much of for years.

Jimmy ran to Henry John, who picked him right up, held him high and said, "Whoa now, my little purple horse, what have you got yourself into now?" Jimmy was covered afresh with raspberry juice from what he'd eaten on the way home. I gave Mama the pail of what was left and showed her the two jars of jam I'd brought home. I couldn't look at her. Couldn't look at either of them.

"I'm taking this up to show Banker," I said, grabbing a jar of jam and slipping out of her reach.

Banker was duly impressed with the jam. I found I couldn't talk to him, as I had vaguely thought I might, and merely wandered around, looking at things, smelling the odor of ink and newspaper that hung heavy in the air. In July, which this was, his room got hot, as did all the upstairs of that house. But he said he didn't mind and sat there day and night, cutting out his finds in perfect coolness. Even Banker looked new to me, suspicious somehow. Was he in on this too in some way I couldn't fathom? I knew he liked Henry John, but then we all did. It never meant anything much before, but now, now I could see what it *might* mean, and I was horrified.

"Let me see your book on murder," I asked Banker. He kept "Murder" separate from "Tragedy," a subtle distinction I was only just then beginning to appreciate. Banker was sitting in his soft chair, reluctant to move.

"It's under the table there, Edda, the brown one. See it? Yes, that's it." It was a large flat photo album, stuck in between others, which were just like it in size but of varying colors—red, green, black, gold.

I pulled it out, took it over to the floor by the window, and sat down. I didn't read the articles; there were too many, and I was too wound up to read. Instead I looked at the pictures, carefully, one by one. I would think, this is the face of a killer, and stare hard into the vacant newsprint eyes of each of the men and women on the pages. Some of the women looked beautiful. One, in faded yellow, was wearing a hat with a feather in it. But the men, the men looked mostly rough, with greasy black hair and T-shirts cut off at the shoulder. That wasn't like Henry John, who always wore clean clothes. There was one man in a fancy black suit wearing a fedora. He was older, not as old as Banker but older than the rest. He didn't look like Henry John either. There were some with mustaches and one with a wild beard and hair down to his shoulders. He had a cross or some kind of tattoo on his forehead. No one had the eyes.

I shut Banker's book and sat still for a minute. A slight breeze had come up, and I let it lift my hair. I was sweaty. Banker let me be; he made no inquiries, no comments. Mama called for me to come set the table, and I stood up to leave.

"I'll take it," Banker said, meaning the book. I handed it to him. "Are you all right, Peachpit? You look kind of worn out."

"Yeah, I'm worn out. See you later." So worn out's what they call it, I thought. I'm worn out. It seemed right. I was.

Now that I could see them and call them by name, I could tell the differences in Mama. Not only was her laugh deeper around him, throatier, but she seemed more animated. She touched her hair a lot. Did she used to do that? I couldn't remember. I saw her looking at him, not directly, not the way she had searched him that night after the funeral, but studying him slyly, shyly looking down and away if he turned and found her eyes on him.

Henry John was just the same as ever, although more so. Mooning is what Annie called it, which was on the mark. Even as I watched them, revolted by them, I could not help feeling just a tiny bit jealous. The only person who had ever looked at me with open-eyed devotion, with flat-out love and undying, undying admiration, had been my father.

Chapter 10

One night several weeks later Jimmy woke up howling holy terror in the middle of the night. Banker didn't even bother to get up anymore, nor did I, although I could hardly sleep through it. We both let Mama take care of it. That night, what time was it really? Midnight? Two o'clock? Henry John came in the room with her. I saw him by the door, his shadow huge and leaping on the wall beside me. Mama picked up Jimmy, who was, as usual, too frightened to open his eyes yet. On her way out the door she bent down, Jimmy heavy in her arms, and smoothed my hair. "Try to go back to sleep, sweetheart," she murmured. In the dark I glared at her.

"What's *he* doing here?" I hissed. She looked over her shoulder and then back at me.

"Go to sleep. We'll talk tomorrow." Henry John walked over and lifted Jimmy from her arms, talking sweetly in a low, easy voice.

"How about if I take this little guy downstairs, Frances?" Mama nodded and sank heavily down onto my bed. Her eyes were shut, and for a long time she just sat there.

"Mama," I ventured, "are you in love with Henry John?" The words felt sticky and unfamiliar in my mouth. Amy Eversole might be "in love" with Bill Peyton, people on TV fell "in love" every night, Mama and Daddy had been "in love," or so they'd said, but none of that seemed close. She sighed deeply and searched her skirt pockets for a cigarette. I was glad she didn't have any.

"In love?" she asked from far away, as though she too understood how strange the idea was. "Edda, I didn't know you even thought about such things."

"Well, I do. I think about a lot more than you know."

"Yes, that I believe. And you want to know if I'm in love with Henry? Is that what you're asking?" I nodded. "Well, I suppose I am, a little. Does that answer your question?"

Suddenly, I couldn't catch my breath. It was as though I had been running fast, running scared a great distance, while in fact I lay still in my warm, rumpled sheets. I was gasping for air. "Oh, Mama." She stretched out her body and lay down beside me, tucking her arm in beneath my head, pulling us close.

"Is it so awful, sweetheart?" she murmured. I began to cry. She stroked my hair and cheek, not talking, just letting me be. After a while she turned over on her back and lay with her arms tucked in behind her head, staring up toward the water stains on the ceiling. From below, we could hear Jimmy shifting down a gear.

"You know, Edda, it's pretty awful to me too," she said.

"I do feel something for him. I feel a lot. He's taken care of us so well since . . . since . . . you know."

"Since he killed Daddy," I spat out.

"Oh, for God's sake!" Her voice was almost a moan. "Are you still onto that? I had no idea." She was crying now but not in her usual way, crying as I had just done, with sounds and hiccups and sobs. "No. What's awful for me, child, is not what people say or think. I know, I know in my heart and in every part of who I am that he didn't kill Ed. Not the way you're thinking, not the way those spiteful old gossips in town or anywhere else might wish to imply." She broke off crying and sat up. I too sat up, not wishing her too far above me.

"What's worse for me is that I *do* love him, love him some, anyway. But I can't let go of Ed enough to feel it, to do him or myself or any of us any good with my love. When your daddy died, we weren't finished; we weren't at a stopping place, not even a place where you could pause and take any comfort from that. I'm still . . . with him, still hoping for things. Oh God! Forget it, Edda, forget all of this. What am I doing talking this way to you, anyway? I know you can't understand this; I don't quite understand it myself. I need a cigarette; wait a minute."

She got up quickly and was gone, leaving behind her only the warm, charged place she'd been. I sat there in the dark, listening, waiting, wired awake with adrenaline. She was right that I didn't understand; I didn't. I very rarely understood my mother, not in the mental sense of that word, but I felt for her, felt her pain and her confusion like a jolt.

She came back in with the dark-orange glow of a cigarette at her side, walking slowly in the dark, holding an ashtray in one hand and groping with the other. She found the bed, sat down, and looked at me straight in the face. My mother's face was pale, almost white in the moonlight shadows. There were dark smudges under the dark-dark place of her eyes, and they looked enormous. "What about you?" she said finally, nodding her head slightly at me. "What is it you're so worried about? Hmm?"

"I don't know," I told her, which was true. "I never even knew what was going on till Annie told me."

"And what exactly did Annie tell you?"

"Well, that he was . . . I don't know. And then you . . . too. You act different, Mama."

"Do I? I'm not surprised. I feel different." She stubbed out her cigarette and put the ashtray on the floor. "You don't hate Henry John, do you, Edda? I don't want you to, but I want to know."

Hate Henry John—did I? "No, I don't hate him. I like him, I guess. It's not that. Mama, really, it's not what he did either. To Daddy I mean. I don't think so anyway. But people will talk, Annie said so, and I can see what she means."

"People talk no matter what. Some people are starved for talk. They'll talk trash and never even know it, or care." This last word she said softly, as a sigh. "People talk, yes, but I hope you won't live your life around other people's talk. That's not the way I want to be, or want you to be either. People's talk can hurt, but when it's idle like that, out of nothing better to do, when they're not people who care about you or even know you, know us, it doesn't matter. You have to shrug it off and go on. Do you understand what I'm saying?"

"Sure." And I did. Mama and Daddy both had preached at me to Be Myself. Banker too. Everybody in my family believed in that. "To thine own self be true." They were family watchwords.

"I know that, Mama. It's more than that."

"What more then?"

"I don't know."

"You don't know or you can't say?"

"I don't know."

She worked her mouth as though she was about to speak, but changed her mind. "Well, go to sleep," she said at last, "I can't tell you how it will all turn out, Edda, what will happen. I'm not sure yet myself. But whatever happens, you won't be losing me. I love you, baby. And your Daddy does too. He goes right on loving you right through death, through time, through it all." Her eyes were streaming now in the old familiar way. "And we go on loving him. No matter what. Okay?" I nodded yes, and she pushed me gently down, pulling the sheets up around me.

That's where we left it for the rest of the summer.

Chapter 11

From what I could observe, love was making both Henry John and Mama stupid. They'd laugh at nothing, just laugh and catch each other's eyes and laugh some more. She seemed to think he was the absolute best fix-it man since the world began. He cleaned out some junk that was in the coal shed and fixed the door on it so you could open and close it without pinching yourself. The way Mama carried on about it a person would have thought he'd just been elected President of the United States. "Oh Henry, it's wonderful. It's just fantastic. I can't believe it."

He was the same way every time he took a meal with us, which was almost every night. "Frances, you're the best. Umm-um. I mean it. What a spread. Oh, this is good." She'd say "Now, Henry," but he would shake his head and eat some more. "I mean it. Delicious." Far as I could tell, the food was just about what it had always been, but then my mouth was spiced with apprehension, not love. Also, she did start making some new dishes, things he remembered from his childhood—Irish stew and apple crisp.

Henry John was an orphan too, like Mama. It was another one of those things, a coincidence, something shared. It seemed to me they counted and polished those "things" like they were pearls on a chain. They'd each got their social security numbers from the same place in Pittsburgh, the East Liberty office, and got them the same year. Maybe they were in there together. "Just think!" they'd say. So I would think: Big deal. They knew the same streets, the same stores, bars, schools. Pittsburgh began to take on a shape, a reality it had never had before. But not really, not for me. What I felt most was left out. They had those places, even people in common, but I didn't. I was Daddy's child; I knew the people he knew, and I lived on where he'd left me. I had no other past to go back to, to start over from.

There were times I suspected her of disloyalty, despite the assurances she had made me that night in the middle of the night. I once heard her tell Annie that she had never in her life felt so well taken care of as she did now by Henry John, so cherished. That was the word she used, and it ground like glass in my ears. I don't know what Annie said back; they were on the phone, and I was eavesdropping, subtly I thought, from the living room, where I was supposedly reading a book. I spied a lot that summer, hanging in shadows and holding still on the stairwell, listening, piecing it together, trying to make it fit.

Banker was no help. I hadn't words to explain my dilemma, and he offered none of his own. In some way Mama seemed to have forgotten Daddy, forgotten Ed Combs and the person she was when she was his wife. But then, when she was alone with me and Jimmy, she talked about him more than ever. "Your daddy was such a good man," she'd say. She told us stories about when we were born, when we were babies, what Daddy thought, what he said, what we said to him.

Jimmy loved to hear how she broke her leg when she was pregnant with him. We could both tell him that story, and we did. "I'm a miracle?" he'd ask when Mama got to the part about what the doctor said. "Oh yes, you are," she'd say, squeezing him into a hug, "most definitely that." When I was born, Daddy'd walked the floors for twenty-five hours. Her labor was long and hard. When I finally got here, at 4:32 in the morning, he rushed to meet the doctor at the delivery room door. He was assured several times that Mama and I were both all right. "Ten fingers?" he'd asked. "Ten toes?" I had all the standard equipment, but he wasn't allowed to see either of us for several more hours. In his excitement and frustration he drove downtown to the newspaper in Lexington, in the middle of the night, and put an ad in the classifieds. WELCOME EDDA COMBS, it says. Banker had it saved of course.

Sometimes she'd talk about just the two of them, of how they met at McDonald's. Jimmy found it awesome to think that his mother had actually worked at McDonald's. There weren't any then in eastern Kentucky, but we'd seen the ads for it on TV, and we'd tasted their food one time on a trip to Cincinnati. Once, when he was very very angry with her—he must have been four or five—Jimmy said in a haughty, cold voice, "Don't think, Mama, just because you worked at McDonald's that you know everything about children." He got even angrier when she burst out laughing, and he wouldn't be mollified until she sobered up and said, very seriously, "I won't." She told us how Daddy had gone to Frankfort to speak to the legislature once about strip mining. She told us too that when they were getting married and the preacher had gotten to the part where you were supposed to say, "I do," he'd looked confused, as if he'd forgotten his part. After a pause, he said, "I reckon." Mama would laugh at that and say, "I reckon that was good enough for me."

In August, Henry John built Mama a picture shelf. It was two shelves really, hung on the living room wall. The wood they were cut from was something fine and dark, polished to a sheen. He was a careful carpenter, and he took his time to make it level and strong. He rounded off the corners so that Jimmy's head wouldn't come to harm streaking by them. Mama pointed that out to Annie one day soon after the shelves were hung.

"Look at this, Annie," she said, touching the smooth beveled edge with her fingers. "He's such a thoughtful man."

"Yeah, it looks good, Fran. Too bad he's not for hire.

Those Cornett boys working at my place are driving me nuts, you wouldn't believe. So what are you going to put here, anyway?"

Mama smiled. "Pictures. They're picture shelves. You'll see when I do it. So will I," she laughed.

Chapter 12

Would Henry John have hammered so hard, cut so carefully, hung those shelves so well, if he'd known what they would hold? I doubt it. For weeks Mama put nothing on them. She would come into the living room, look at them, run her dustcloth over their already shining surfaces, and sit back, in a chair or maybe on the floor, and just look at them some more. They were beautiful, true, but how far can you go on about blank shelves? Mama went the limit.

"I'm just crazy about these shelves, Edda." She must have said it fifty times. No kidding. While they were still empty, she taught Jimmy not to swing on them. We all walked by them several times a day, day after day, absorbing their clean, blank symmetry. I don't think it ever occurred to me to offer her any ideas for what to put on them. They were obviously hers from the word go, a gift from Henry John. She distinguished them from the other work he did around that house because they were "extra"; they were beautiful, and beauty was special. So she said.

"I need something beautiful just now," she told us one

night when we were all gathered in the kitchen. Annie was there, and Henry John of course. "Not that there isn't plenty," she said smiling at each one of us very slightly, slowly, "but I need more. This is my chance to impose."

Annie cocked her head toward Mama from inside the refrigerator door. "What are you talking about, Frances? Impose what? I think this is the last beer—you want to split it, Henry John?" He signaled yes, and she brought two glasses and a sweaty-cold green bottle of beer to the table.

"Impose myself," Mama said. She was sitting at the table, looking out the window. "What I'm best at, if I may say so, is not creating but appreciating. You paint, Annie. And Henry, you play. What do I do?" She turned away from the glass and looked at each of them. She glanced at me, and we smiled at each other.

Nobody said anything so I said, "What? What do you do?"

"I take it in." She spoke solemnly. "I guess there's nothing wrong with that. Somebody's got to or what's the use of it? But still, there's something missing. I want to be creating too." Mama laughed then and looked down at her fingers, which she was lacing and unlacing on the tabletop. "This all sounds much too far flung for what I mean. Highfalutin, as Banker would say. And be right."

"Well, you've created two children, which is more than Henry John or I, or Banker for that matter, has ever done," Annie said.

"Oh, well, that doesn't count," Mama said. "I didn't really *create* these two. I mean I can't take credit for them. Much as I'd like to," she said, reaching down and scruffing Jimmy's golden little head. He climbed up on her lap. "And besides," she added, "most of what I do with them is try *not* to impose, beyond teaching them manners."

"Well, what are you going to put up there?" Annie asked. The shelves had hung empty for several weeks by now. For a person who'd lived in an unfinished house for over three years, Annie was oddly uncomfortable with things unfinished or undone at our house.

"Pictures," Mama said, spreading her hands as though to show us, "like I've said all along, and beautiful things. I'm just not sure yet."

"Maybe you've got creator's block," Henry John joked. He had little beer flecks on his mustache.

"I suppose it could be that," Mama answered straight as a nail. "Do you get blocked like that, Annie, when you go to paint something?"

"Sometimes. I usually know *what* I'm going to paint, but I get stuck sometimes figuring out how. That's what I use sketches for, to fool around with it till I find what I'm looking for."

"Is it like that with you, Henry?" Mama asked.

"Well, not if I'm playing other people's stuff. That's a whole different block, performer's block. And with the songs I write myself, they often just come to me fully written when I'm brushing my teeth or driving around. But yes, there're times when I want to write something, I want a song for what's in me, and I can't get it. I can strain and strain for it, but that doesn't mean I'll get it."

Mama was nodding, listening carefully, brushing her face lightly from time to time in Jimmy's curls, resting her chin on his head. "Well, I don't think I'm having creator's block after all. I'm just considering. And enjoying the structure itself. There aren't many things man-made around here that you can point to and say, 'This is beautiful, straight, and true.' "

"You've seen my living room," Annie said with a mock groan. "I don't believe there's a straight board in that place. And you know the trouble I've had with finding help. There's a different work ethic or standard of workmanship here than I've ever seen."

"There's *no* standard of workmanship here," Henry John said with unusual force. "Those stereotypes about hillbillies didn't just materialize out of thin air. I have never seen such sloth, such total disregard for a job well done as there is here in eastern Kentucky."

"Now, Henry," Mama said, glancing anxiously at me, "I don't think that's quite fair."

"It's fair all right, Frances. Look at your own house. Annie's place at least has the excuse of age. But this place, this place was built no more than twenty years ago, and it's a mess. It was never built to hold out the weather, never built to stand up straight. And what's worse"—he was really angry—"what galls me no end, is there is no excuse for it.

Chances are, the people who built this house lived here first. It wasn't like some of these construction crews up in cities where they build two hundred units in a month in some subdivision. This was their house; they lived here, am I right? And they still didn't care, didn't take the time to do it well. It's unbelievable."

We all looked at him in silence. This outburst was uncharacteristic. I had rarely heard him say so much at one time and never with such feeling. Even Henry John himself seemed to think some explanation was called for. He continued in a voice that was almost apologetic. "We grew up in a house in Pittsburgh, lived there until my parents died . . . My father was a bricklayer. A master. He cared so much. He always told us that. Do a good job, make it straight, lay it right. We grew up in a house in Pittsburgh." He smiled at my mother. "Nothing fancy, not fancy at all. But brick, three solid floors of it, and plaster and paint and wood to match. It was built to last. And made beautiful too. Not gorgeous, mind you, but little touches here and there, molding on the wood, tile near the fireplace, one stained glass window that was my mother's pride and joy." He shook his head. "I miss it."

"So why do you stay here if you hate it so much?" Annie asked with an edge in her voice.

"Oh," he looked uneasy, even red, "I just do." He looked at Mama. "Don't we all?"

Mama laughed. "I guess that's to the point. We're a little colony of outsiders, my children excepted, and they're what

Annie here calls half-breeds. I find it hard to make judgments about things here. There's so much I feel excluded from, it's hard to know all the reasons for the way things are, the way they're done and not done. And I'm afraid that we may be just as excluding in our own way as the natives are of us."

"I don't feel excluded, Frances," Annie said sharply. "I think the mountain people make up in warmth what they lack in straight edges. And Henry John, there are reasons, historical reasons, for the way things are here. Try not to forget it. This county right here had the next to the highest infant mortality rate in the country last year. Only place that was worse was some Indian reservation. This is poor country, and it's been poor a long time."

"What's infant mortality rate?" I asked—which was a mistake because it made Mama notice me, notice Jimmy too, even though he had been on her lap, and made her think about bedtime.

"It's when babies die, Edda," Annie explained.

"Good Lord!" Mama said, "It's eight thirty. Come on, boy, time for you to go up. Edda, fifteen minutes."

"Twenty, please?" I wheedled. I loved staying up past Jimmy. She had agreed that I could, being older and all, but we never settled just how much. School had started back, but since I was in the fifth grade, I didn't have to turn the light out till nine. She'd let me go longer if I was in the middle of a good chapter and I'd swear to quit as soon as I finished.

"You're going to cut down your reading time," Mama said.

"It's okay."

"Your choice." She shrugged and got up, putting Jimmy on the floor. "Time to go upstairs to bed. Say good night."

Jimmy gave Henry John a big hug around his neck and said, "Carry me." Henry John scooped him up in one smooth, swift motion, and they were gone. Mama smiled. "Fifteen minutes, girl," she said and followed them out. It was still in the kitchen then. Annie sat across the table from me, her glass empty, eyeing me. I felt uncomfortable. I wanted them all back, talking their grown-up talk that I found so incomprehensible and yet so interesting. I'd avoided being alone with Annie since that day in early summer when she told me what was what about Henry John and Mama.

"So how are you, Miss Combs?" she asked with play formality. I shrugged.

"Fine. You?" I asked, politely as I could.

"Do you like him?" she said suddenly, pointedly, ignoring my manners.

"He's okay." I could feel her looking at me, but I couldn't look up.

"So how's school?" she said after a pause, and I could tell by her tone she'd dismissed me somehow.

"Terrible. The usual." I dismissed her back.

Just then I heard, with relief, Henry John clattering back down the stairs. He resumed his conversation with Annie as though it had never been interrupted. "There's poverty everywhere, Annie. My mother was born on the boat coming

over here; her people were starving to death in Ireland. My
father too was first generation. We came from poor people;
we were poor a long time ourselves. I'm talking more than
poor. I'm talking about sloth, laziness."

"You're looking at depression and calling it by meaner
names," Annie said. "And besides, there's craftsmanship
here. Surely you've seen the baskets, the quilts, the rocking
chairs. Are you saying that doesn't count or that it's not
up to your high Irish standards?"

They locked eyes. Henry John answered, "Neither. Both.
I'm saying there's too damned little of it. What kind of
people throw their garbage in the creek and then turn around
and tell you how much they love their mountain home?"

"Exactly the same kind of people that burn down their
own homes and loot their own stores. Poor people. People
who can't take it anymore. Rioting is acting out. Here
they're past that stage; they're too exhausted to be angry.
It's an acting in, if you will. Or a sinking in perhaps. That's
despair you see, Henry John."

"Now wait a minute. There's plenty of new money in
here these days. Coal's in a boom. You ought to come up
on one of these jobs with me someday if you doubt that.
It's unbelievable what they're taking out of here. And don't
tell me all the money's going to the big industrialists somewhere else, because it's not. There's money here all right.
But look what they do with it. Look at that new house
going up on Highway 12. Purple siding? Who is this guy
with his purple siding? And gold shutters yet, too."

"The nouveau riche are notorious for garishness, Henry

John, so what? In America if you have the bucks, you have the very same right as they do to be obnoxious in your own way." I made a note to look up *nouveau riche* in my dictionary, but I couldn't find it. I guess I was spelling it wrong.

"Okay, Annie, you can flash your Vassar education all you want. You can feel sorry for them and make excuses, but I won't treat them that way. Nine chances out of ten, for all his big bucks and bad taste Mr. Rich Man can't find somebody to put in a decent job of plumbing any better than you can, with all your good taste. The know-how for it just doesn't exist around here. Nor the patience to learn how and do it right."

"You're proving my point," Annie said coolly.

"Well, I sure as hell don't mean to," Henry John said hotly. "I don't agree with your point. I think it's condescending. People here could do better if they tried. 'Don't work too hard,' people say, as if a little hard work would do them any harm. Making mistakes, doing a sloppy job has almost been given the status of a virtue."

Slowly, drawing out each syllable so that the words seemed to hang, to sway in the air, Annie said, "Nobody's perfect." I knew with a sick, sudden shock that she was referring to Henry John's "mistake." He knew it too, for without meaning to, our eyes met for one wretched, frightened moment. Wide-eyed he was, and hurt. He looked then at Annie, who sat smiling at him, smirking almost, and then he looked down.

"No, you're right," he said in a low, lost voice, addressing the floor, "nobody's perfect."

106·

I sat frozen in the silence that followed. Mama called down just then for me to come up. Without argument I slid out of my chair and said good night to both of them. Passing Henry John, I reached out and touched him ever so slightly on the knee. He was still looking down and did not look up, but he made a slight motion with one of his hands as though to touch me back. They were still not talking when I left the room.

What I felt for him was pity, a strange emotion for me. He looked in that brief second like the Henry John I'd met that first night after Daddy died. Gone was the filled-out, fattened-up, jollier version of himself that had been spending so much time around the house. She'd knocked away his confidence with one swift blow. And then, what Mama did with those shelves finished him off.

Chapter 13

Banker was the keeper of the family records, what archives we Combses could lay claim to, which weren't many. Mama went to him and asked to look at the pictures. He had a whole box full of nothing but pictures. She kept telling him to go downstairs and look at the shelves. She was always on him to get out more. But Banker wasn't sick, just stationary. He said when she got them done he'd come downstairs and have a look. In the meantime he handed her over the box of pictures, and she proceeded to lose herself in it.

Literally. She'd pick Jimmy and me up at Mrs. Stumbo's after work and bring us home. Then upstairs to her room she'd go, leaving us to our own devices, which usually amounted to TV, until we got hungry and went upstairs looking for her. Day after day we found her on her bed, with photographs flowing out under her like a new quilt. Or a shroud. She'd be back up there right after dinner and late into the night.

She told Henry John not to come over, "till she got it done," but then I'd hear her talking to him late at night, her voice wavery and full of tears. She asked Jimmy and me to be patient with her, please. I think we were. She said, "This isn't going to last forever, but I do need to get these shelves fixed." Everyone waited. Mama was always crying when we'd go in to see her, not even sad, but streaming tears more than ever, which had already been more than average—had been since Daddy's death, which was then almost exactly two years previous.

I don't know if Mama was aware of the anniversary. She never mentioned it if she was. I wasn't. Not really. I knew it was late September. And I knew when Daddy had died—September 30—but it wasn't something I thought about all the time. I don't even know if I would've noticed it at all if Henry John hadn't yelled it at her that night they got into such a fight.

September 30 was the day she put her pictures up, the ones she had chosen. Jimmy and I were shooed up to our room and told to clean it.

We picked up a few things. I looked in the mirror and thought about Mama's shelves. This was in the evening, and she'd made a big deal about it at dinner, that all she had left to do was put the stuff on. Then we could all come down, Banker included.

I went into Mama's room, looking for clues. What for weeks had been chaos was completely cleaned up. The pictures she hadn't chosen were back in their box. She'd had pictures tacked up everywhere in there—on lampshades, her mirror, the walls, the bedposts. Mostly they were baby pictures of Jimmy and me. But now they were gone.

Finally she called upstairs, and Jimmy went running

down. He probably thought it was Christmas or something from the way Mama had built it up. I went in to Banker, who was just then slowly lifting himself out of his chair. "Banker, what's this all about?" I asked him. "Do you know?"

"Hmm. Do I know?" He considered this as he did nearly everything, evenly. "No, Edda, I can't say that I do, beyond what you know and Frances knows that she's told us, which is that she wants some pretty picture shelves. Anything wrong with that, my suspicious relative?" He was smiling at me.

"No. Not exactly. I've just got a creepy feeling, Banker."

"Oh-ho. Now, this could be a case of female intuition. Do you know what that is?"

"What?"

"It's when ladies get absolutely spooky about things and they can't explain it, but there it is. Are you spooky about this or just creepy?"

"Banker, go on. Are you serious?" I couldn't tell.

"Well," he said, backing off, chuckling a little, "maybe you better ask your mother about it—woman to woman, that sort of thing. I'm afraid I really don't know much about it. But it's plenty well known about."

"What is it again?" I asked. Maybe I could look it up.

"Female intuition. Some people call it women's intuition, but I believe girl children get it too. Ask your mama. Come on. Let's go see what Frances has come up with."

I walked down the steps behind him, using his sloping

back as a shield. Why was I so uneasy? Downstairs Mama was holding Jimmy up so he could see each picture, putting names to the faces. He was squinting at them, studying. She looked up when we came in and said, "Here they are. I hope you like it."

And there were her pictures, perhaps twenty of them: some very old in sepia, some in color, some black and white. In between them she'd laid several seashells, a Chinese vase she said we mustn't touch, and a few sprigs of fall flowers. There was also a marble as I recall, oversize, green, and glowing. This was her collection, her imposition, her creation. And it *was* pretty. Light bounced off the polished wood, the silver frames, reflecting upward into the people's faces.

There was a couple just stepping into a large old-fashioned sedan. The man was very dark and wore a hat. He looked like a gangster. The woman was smiling. Her lips looked black, and her hair was short, framing her face. She was wearing a gown. Those were Mama's parents on their wedding day. I'd never seen them before.

There was a picture of Banker—that's what they said, but I never could quite believe it—at the age of eight. He was wearing knickers with suspenders and high buckle shoes; his hair was plastered down, and he was smiling, big. How could Banker ever be that boy? Behind him rose the first slope of a mountain.

There was a picture of Mamaw and Papaw, Daddy's parents. They were sitting against a backdrop of paneling;

Papaw was standing with one hand on Mamaw's shoulder. Neither one was smiling, just staring out. We'd hardly ever seen them since Daddy died. One time they just showed up. It was a Saturday, and Mamaw said to Mama, "Since you're not going to come see us, we thought we'd pay you a call." They'd stayed all day and never smiled, never once sat back in a chair. I remember the hard, clean smell of Mamaw as I bent over her to lay a careful kiss on her stiff, dry cheek. They had a bumper sticker on their car that read: "God said it, I believe it, and that settles it." When they'd driven off that night, Mama stood a long time at the gate looking out at the dust on the road that had been kicked up by their leaving.

There were lots of pictures of Daddy. I guess my favorite was one in which he's holding me, and I'm a tiny baby, holding me up to look at some spheres hanging in a window. Mama said it was a mobile they'd bought for me—of the planets, I think. I look just like a baby, way up in the air, studying these things. Daddy's looking up at me; his arms are outstretched, and his face looks real soft and kind of awestruck. I can't remember it of course; I was only about six months old, but I can remember that expression on him.

There was one real hard-to-see picture of Daddy holding Jimmy, right after he'd been born. Daddy looks huge, massive, and Jimmy is just a little bundle of blankets. But even through paper you can feel the tenderness of his touch. It's like Jimmy is the most precious thing in the world; he's holding him that way.

There was one of Mama and Daddy standing outside the golden arches of McDonald's in New York City. They're both making funny faces like the sun was in their eyes. Her hair is shorter than I've ever seen it, really curly, and they've got their arms wrapped around each other. They look so different in that picture; it's hard to say how. More than younger.

There was one of Daddy in his soldier uniform, real serious, standing with some other guys Mama said were friends of his. Nobody's smiling. It was taken in a jungle somewhere, and the light in it is softer and greener than any light I've ever seen.

One picture I begged her and begged her to take down, but she wouldn't. It was of me and Jimmy sitting barenaked in a bathtub. He's just a little squirt of a thing, but I must be seven. I remember Daddy taking that picture, looming in the bathroom, saying, "Say cheese. Say whiskey. Smile, youall. Come on." And we're smiling all right. Naked. Mama said I was being silly, but I said I noticed there weren't any naked pictures of *her* up there.

There was a close-up shot of Jimmy as a newborn. His face is red and smooth and kind of puffy. His eyes are absolutely black black and real misty-looking. It's like he's thinking very hard about something, really thinking. "Fresh from the source" is what Mama called that.

So many faces, caught in time, held there on her shelves among the seashells and the flowers. Those faces looked out at us for years.

After a while Banker stood back and put his arm around Mama. "It's lovely, Frances, a truly lovely thing."

"I'm glad you like it, Banker," she said, wiping her eyes. "I'm satisfied somehow. It feels good to have it up." They stood quietly together, looking at the shelves. "So," she said, putting on a hearty tone, "since you're down and gracing the living room with your presence, how about a cup of chocolate? We can sit in here a while. I called Henry, and he's coming by in a bit. How about it? I'd like it if you would."

"I'd be delighted."

"With marshmallows?" Jimmy asked, taking the question out of my mouth.

"The works," Mama said. "I feel like a little party." We were sitting there drinking chocolate when Henry John came in. Mama got right up and met him at the door. They kissed each other on the cheek. I could remember her kissing Daddy just that same way, and I felt again what was by then a familiar pang.

She led him by the hand over to the shelves. There was something shy about both of them. He stood there a long time, taking in what she had done. "Do you like it?" she asked at last, her voice high and thin. He nodded but did not speak. He kept on looking.

Late that night I heard them yelling. Jimmy never did wake up, which is just as well. I slipped out on the hall landing and sat there shivering in my nightgown, although the night was warm.

"It's a goddammed shrine is what it is," I heard Henry John yell.

"Don't you speak to me that way," Mama came back at him. "How dare you? I needed to make something, some family. Is that so bad? Can't you understand that? I'm trying to find my family, what's left of them." Her voice was rougher than I'd ever heard it. This was scary.

"I want to marry you, Frances," Henry John roared. "Can you get *that* through your thick skull? *I* want to be your family." I realized then that he was crying. I wondered what he looked like crying. There were mumbles and things I couldn't hear, only the sound of their voices running up and down scales, like Amy Eversole practicing her piano.

At some point it got very quiet, deathly still down there. It was a physical effort not to creep down and look. But then, rising up clearly, like a bell, I heard Mama say, "I can't, Henry. I can't. I'm still married to Ed."

"Ed Combs is dead," Henry John answered. "No one knows that better than I. He's been dead two years tonight, Frances. Tonight. I want to take you out of here."

Again they were mumbling, talking so softly I couldn't make out the words. But then something crashed, broke, shattered. "Then why the hell have you been leading me on?" I heard him say. He was screaming it practically.

"Is that what you call it?" Mama yelled. "Well, consider yourself unled. Damn you, Henry John Fitzpatrick. God-damn your very eyes." I had never heard her talk like that.

"You can rot here then. Lie down with the dead on Cauley's Creek if that's how you want it."

"Yes. Yes. That's how I want it. Now get out. Get out and don't you come back. Do you hear me?" Her voice was breaking, she was sobbing. The door slammed, and I could hear Henry John gun the motor on his truck. He burned rubber leaving there that night, tearing off. Downstairs I heard Mama crying, deep, heaving, horrible sobs.

Suddenly, someone touched my shoulder and I jumped. It was Banker, standing over me in the dark, looking like a ghost. He never said a word, and I didn't either. He helped me up though and steered me back to my bed. He stood in the doorway watching as I pulled sheets and blankets up under my chin. I was shivering bad. Then he went back to his room, and I lay there listening for a long, long time to Mama's pain.

Chapter 14

Henry John left. He went up to Lexington and got a job as a surveyor with some engineering firm. I heard that from Annie. Mama wouldn't say much about it, just "He's gone." She went around red-eyed and drawn down into herself for what seemed to me a long time. She quit telling funny stories at dinner, and for a while I tried to take it over, but I wasn't very good at it. I'm just not all that funny.

At Christmas that year Henry John sent me *The Lion, the Witch, and the Wardrobe*, and the note inside said, "From one dreamer to another." To my surprise, I missed him. I know Jimmy did because he'd ask about him over and over, till Mama would start crying and leave the room, and I'd have to tell him to hush. He couldn't understand about people disappearing, and I couldn't think of any way to explain it.

In some way I felt guilty, like it was me that had driven him off. Me and Annie. I kept thinking she had something to do with it too, even though I knew she didn't. Annie didn't act real happy about him being gone; nobody did.

For one thing, Mama was so sad it was hard to be happy at all. But inside, when I'd be at school or down the creek at Heaven alone, I'd get this sense of satisfaction like "job well done"; and it scared me, like maybe I'd made it happen after all. Annie would come over in the evening sometimes and sit with Mama. I would hear them talking about "men," and I'd try to listen in, learn something. But Mama had caught on by then to my spying ways because she'd shoo me out. For a long time I thought about Henry John, and then I just quit.

We lived on about like before; at some point I realized that I could hardly recall his face, and I didn't care. In the spring Mama planted her garden in the spot that he'd dug up for her by the kitchen door. The bigger garden that Daddy'd worked when he was alive lay fallow. Mama said it was too much for just us.

Amy Eversole kissed Bill Peyton, or he kissed her; it was hard to tell from the story she told, although I heard it at least a hundred times. She quit the daredevil club at Mrs. Stumbo's, which left me in it alone; Jimmy was still too young, and the Piper twins were too mean to fool with. And too young anyway. Jimmy was even younger, but at least he had sense. I was eleven going on twelve. No matter how far till my next birthday, I was always going on the next age. I did that all the way up to twenty-one, which was last year, and then I was finally able to slow down. When I was a teenager I'd just flat out lie about my age. I said I was eighteen for four years before I ever was. But that year, when I was eleven, I met a boy I liked. I didn't love him, mind you, I didn't have a crush either. But I liked him in what I knew, even then, was a special way.

His name was Charlie Henson. His family had just moved back from up in Akron. There was work that year in Spence, jobs in the mines and elsewhere; lots of people were moving in, moving back. (For a while it looked like we were going to have to move. Our landlord's son and his family were coming home, but at the last minute they found a house in town that they preferred to living up Cauley's Creek.)

Charlie was one of those people who can do enormous math problems in their heads in a matter of seconds. When they first found out about it at school, Mrs. Hawthorn, our math teacher, accused him of using a calculator, but he wasn't. Then she made a big deal about it and had him show off in front of the class and other teachers even. After a while he got so he wouldn't do it. He just acted like he couldn't, but I knew that he was just tired of being fussed over. Sometimes when she was talking about him, he'd be sitting right behind her back or somewhere just enough out of sight so she wouldn't see the faces he was making while she yapped. But I'd see them, and I'd laugh, and after a while I came to like him a lot.

He lived on a block in town not far from Mrs. Stumbo's. We'd walk over there together, and sometimes he'd come in or we'd sit out back together, and he'd help me with my math homework. Charlie was my friend. In a way I felt closer to him than to Amy, although I still saw her more.

She had suddenly gone totally goofy about stuff I didn't care about: fingernail polish, training bras, deodorant. When she "finally" got her period, she acted like she was the queen of England or something. She made me feel like I was about five years old because I was totally flat-chested and nowhere near getting mine. (Her sister Andrea once said I wasn't just flat-chested, I was inverted. Ha ha.)

Charlie and I could talk. He liked to talk about stars and space and black holes and quasars—stuff like that. I liked to listen to it; he made it all sound so possible, huge but manageable. For my part I talked about Earth. I loved to look in magazines and see pictures of places I'd never been to, think about going there, living there. I had a sense of how many people there are in the world, how many lives there were being lived that I knew nothing about.

I talked to Charlie about hunger too. It plagued me bad that there could be so many people starving to death out there. I'd seen a show about it on TV and asked Mama if it was true. She said yes, it was, had been forever. I couldn't believe it. I hated it. When I first found out about it, I couldn't understand why it wasn't solved immediately. It seemed perfectly simple to me.

Perfectly. I put on a backyard carnival at Mrs. Stumbo's one day that summer. Charlie helped me make signs and think up ideas. He even manned a booth, doing "Amazing Math Problems" for a dime. Annie helped too; she sat for half a day and let kids throw wet sponges at her. Mama brought lemonade and cups and cookies. Jimmy and Mrs.

Stumbo sold them every one; and then Mrs. Stumbo brought out more, and we sold them too. We made twenty-eight dollars that day and sent it off to CARE. Mama looked up the address. I knew it wasn't that much money, but in their letter back CARE said it bought all kinds of milk and tools for making a well or something in India. I felt good about that, but then they'd send me more letters, and every one of them had pictures in it of babies bloated with hunger or corpses on a dusty road, and I didn't have any more money to send. It was discouraging.

Charlie used to like to come out to the house. For one thing, he liked Mama. She'd get on talking in that way she had, and he'd look at her like she personally had been the one to hang the moon. She was the only grown-up he knew that he was allowed to call by her first name. He couldn't sleep over—we were too old for that already, him being a boy—but his father would drive him out sometimes on Saturdays, and he'd stay all day.

He's the only boy I ever took to Heaven, the only person at all besides me who'd ever been there, except for Daddy. The first time we went, and we'd crossed that last stretch of rocks and made the turn and there it was, he'd stopped right there and looked around. "I see what you mean, Edda," is what he said, and he did. He saw it the same way I did—Heaven. Charlie and I liked to talk, but it was good to be quiet with him too. Not for years did I realize what a rare thing that was between us.

Toward the end of that summer Mama took Jimmy and

me to the beach. Banker didn't want to go, said he'd seen all the ocean he intended to see back when he was in the navy; said he'd be fine, and besides, Annie would check on him. Mama said she *had* to go, to keep her sanity. Besides, according to her, it was practically a crime against God Himself that I was eleven years old and had never seen the ocean. So we went.

Mama was more excited planning that trip, more talkative than we'd seen her for months or maybe years. She'd arranged with Mr. Robinson for ten days off. I know it was an expensive trip because she fretted some about the money, although not in the gloomy way I'd seen her fret over bills before. She had rented us a house in a little place called Sandbridge, just south of Virginia Beach and Norfolk in Virginia. "It costs more to get a house right on the ocean," she told me. "You can get them cheaper across the street. But I figure, since we're going to do this, let's do it right. This way we can hear it all night long." She'd get so excited thinking about it she would jump up and down and laugh out loud. She and Jimmy made up a little song they sang for two full days in the car. "We're going to the beach, we're going to the beach, we're going going going going going to the beach." There were verses in it too—about sand, sun, water, wind, and who knows what—but that refrain is all I remember.

The trip was long and hot. I sat in the backseat and read until I'd get dizzy, then look out the window for hours at a time. It was strange to be zooming along past people's houses, so many of them, and we never knew a thing about them. I'd see a woman standing in her yard and wonder, Who are you? Mama said I was a good traveler, meaning I was quiet and didn't ask for food every fifteen minutes the way Jimmy did. She never knew how lonesome traveling made me feel.

When we finally got there, topped the last rise and saw the Atlantic Ocean stretching out blue and forever before us, Mama started crying, blubbering. "We made it! Oh, look! Oh, thank you, thank you, God." She pulled the car over, and we all got out.

Jimmy and I both felt cautious; the sand was hot and the smell of the salted wind was strong in our throats. We held hands and picked our way down the dune, following Mama, who had run ahead and plunged, completely clothed, into the breaking waves. She was rolling around in them, laughing like a maniac. When she saw us, she sat up. Her skirt was soaked, and so was her blouse. She held her arms out to us, and we too went in, giggling with the coldness of it, the shock, the newness. She held us in her arms, all three of us buffeted and rocked by the waves, and whispered over and over, "We made it. We're here. At last." When she finally climbed the steps to the real estate office to claim the keys to our beach house, she was soaked to the skin and beaming.

It was fun living in someone else's house. Their furniture, their pictures, even their dishes in the kitchen seemed special to me. As Mama promised, we could hear the ocean in our sleep, a gentle roar. "It gives me great comfort," she told us, "to know that while we're living our lives elsewhere, the ocean is here, day in and night out, year after year, forever." She tried to make a tape recording of the sound of it, something to listen to back home, but it didn't come out. Mama was at peace there, and more. She was happy. This was her Heaven.

We ate shrimp and steamed crabs. One night we sat on the porch and watched a tremendous storm roll in. The next morning the waves were so high and rough that Jimmy almost drowned. He cried, and Mama sat on the sand with him, holding him for a long time. I loved it rough; I wanted it even wilder yet. I'd scream and jump, pound on the water, tumble over, and scramble up to do it again. What a relief to be in an element stronger by far than myself. No rage of mine could touch it, nothing I could do would make it change. Mama watched me and smiled.

The night before we left she took us for a walk on the beach under the moon and the stars. She pointed out Venus and various constellations. I thought about Charlie. She told us a story about how one time she and Daddy had come to the beach, this very one, with no money. They'd slept in the car and drunk gin and eaten crabs. She said gin was nasty stuff, but it was okay at the beach. Jimmy looked at the sky and listened to her talk.

"Daddy?" he asked, pointing to a star.

"Maybe," Mama told him.

Chapter 15

Cauley's Creek looked different to me after that, tame some-how, and smaller. There were problems with the house waiting for us when we got home. The roof in Banker's room was leaking, staining the wallpaper, and one of the porch steps had rotted all the way through.

"I'm no good at this," Mama told Annie one day. They'd been trying to nail a new step down. "Ed wasn't any good at it either, but he at least would have fixed it somehow."

"And been accused of hillbilly workmanship," Annie re-plied, swatting at the step with her hammer.

They were both sweating; Mama had her hair tied up in a scarf. She sighed then.

"Sometimes I miss him," she said, and I knew she meant Henry John, knew it beyond doubt, in a flash. I hadn't thought about him for a long time. "But it wouldn't have been right to marry someone for the convenience of it, now would it?" she asked Annie.

"People marry for far stranger reasons than that, Frances.

But then, you're the moral type, aren't you?" They both laughed at that.

"I guess I am." Mama said, and I wondererd what it meant.

When school started back, I didn't see much of Charlie. He was in the smart class; I was in the other one. The tracking system at Spence Elementary was simple: 1's and 2's. He was a 1, I was a 2. We started having a class called Current Events that year, and I did real well in it, thanks to Banker, who taught me how to read the newspaper. "Spread it out on the floor, take up all the room you need, and scan it first," he told me. His mother had been a seamstress, and she'd let him, as a child, spread the paper out like it was a dress pattern to be cut. He showed me how to read the columns, how to look for world news first, then national, state, and local. His subscription to the Sunday *New York Times* continued to come, week after week, year after year, and it was that paper he told me to study. He also took the Louisville *Courier Journal*, but he said he didn't like it so well as he once did.

Jimmy started kindergarten that year. The first day his hand was sweating in mine as we walked up the cement steps to the school. He was so scared.

"But I don't know how to read," he said. He'd said this over and over, and no amount of reassurance seemed to help.

"Jimmy, you don't have to know how to read in kindergarten," I told him again. "And besides, that's why you *go* to school in the first place. They're going to teach you. I didn't know how to read when I started."

"Yes, you did," he accused, lowering this bit of family lore on me like a boom. Mama sometimes bragged that I could read when I was three years old, but it wasn't true. I guess I could pick out a few words, and she blew it up like it was something wonderful. Jimmy couldn't read at all.

"I don't know how to do homework," he added, although I'd told him plenty there wasn't homework in kindergarten. Mama had to be at work early, so she wasn't with him like she'd been with me when I started Spence. It was up to me to help him through it, and I wasn't doing him much good. But after the first few days he was fine—better than fine; he loved it. Jimmy made friends easily because he always suspected the best of people, even teachers. It was a gift I never had.

Sometime around Thanksgiving, Mama got a letter from Henry John saying he was going to be married. He'd been gone a little over a year. She read it to us out loud at supper. "Why, listen to this," she said in a voice bright and hard with false cheer. She made out like he was just somebody we once knew, nobody in particular, some distant friend. "What do you know about that?" she asked us, as if we could know anything about it at all. "He says this woman is a dancer. A dancer! Imagine that. I'll bet she's beautiful. Dancers always are. He sends his love to you all as usual." She got up then from the table, abruptly, and left the room.

"Who's Henry John?" Jimmy whispered to me.

"Jimmy, you remember, don't you?"

He knitted his brow. "Sort of. I guess I do." He sounded unsure.

Mama was in the living room, looking at her picture shelves, running her hand along the smooth edges of the wood. There was distance in her; she was gone again, somewhere we couldn't follow. But she didn't stay gone that time, not long. I heard her up in Banker's room a few days afterward, talking about it, heard Henry John's name, heard her crying in there. Later, she was okay again. A little sad, but Mama always was a *little* sad.

And then all hell broke loose. How can I explain it? Even now it seems like a bad dream we couldn't wake up from. Maybe that sounds corny, or cliché, but it's true. It started without warning one day at school, during lunch break. I was out on the playground doing what I always did at recess—nothing. Otis Spicer, a boy in my class, came up to me and said, "Your daddy had V.D." Just like that. Otis was always bothering the girls, snapping bra straps and peeking up skirts, or trying to. I'd learned long ago to ignore him, but this was something different, something new, something about my father.

"What?" I asked him.

"I said, your daddy had V.D." He was sneering at me with his big ugly, yellow, crooked teeth. I didn't know what V.D. was exactly, but I knew it was something bad.

"He did not."

"He did too, and he got it from that hippie lady." That meant Annie; she was often referred to that way by people who didn't know her.

"He did not," I screamed at Otis, and then I jumped him. I don't know how or why or what possessed me, but I jumped him hard and had him down on the ground before he knew it. I was sitting on his chest and hitting him in the face. With my fists yet. "Don't you talk like that about my daddy," I screamed at him, was screaming still when two teachers came over and pulled me off.

Fighting in school was bad enough, but to be a girl, in the sixth grade, fighting a boy and beating him was a mark, a brand, I would never live down. If I know Spence, there are people there who talk about it to this day. Through a blur of pure red rage and furious tears I saw their faces as I was marched off the playground and into the principal's office. I saw Amy gaping at me and turning away. I saw Charlie's puzzled stare, saw fingers pointing and hands covering mouths. I heard the giggles and the gasps, heard their whispers for weeks to come, and then read them in their eyes for weeks after that.

I sat mute in Mrs. Patterson's office, unable to explain myself. I would not repeat Otis Spicer's words, could make no excuse for my "behavior," as Mrs. Patterson called it. I was so angry still, sitting in that hard wooden chair that I could not catch my breath, unclench my jaw, or loosen my fists. They called Mama.

She came running into the office looking panic-stricken,

her high heels clattering unevenly as she limp-ran all the way down the hall. I was sitting there, breathing slower but still speechless. Ignoring Mrs. Patterson, who was standing over me, Mama fell to her knees in front of my chair and stared hard, hard into my face.

"Edda, are you all right?" I could not even nod.

"Mrs. Combs"—Mrs. Patterson addressed her from some height—"Edda is hardly the injured party."

Mama kept staring at me, put her hand to my cheek. "I was so worried, on the phone." She was talking to me, not Mrs. Patterson. "Are you all right?" she asked again. This time I managed to blink. I was worried for her. Nobody ignored Mrs. Patterson and lived to tell the tale, and here Mama was, on the floor, acting like there was no one else in the room but me.

She looked up at Mrs. Patterson, who was a long, thin, gray woman with a pinched mouth and tiny piercing gray eyes. Mama collected herself and got up, glancing at me repeatedly.

"Hello, I'm Mrs. Combs," she said politely, offering her hand to Mrs. Patterson, which seemed an almost ridiculous gesture. "We've met before, but of course you meet so many people." She was rambling. Mrs. Patterson ignored her hand.

"I know who you are," she said ominously. "And I would assume, from what we said on the phone, that you know why I called. Edda was fighting in the schoolyard. With a boy. She is quite unhurt, as you can see. The boy, however, may have a broken nose." This was the first I'd heard of that possibility. Good, I thought.

"Well"—Mama sounded breathless—"I guess I'm a bit of a worry wart. You know. I didn't know what to think. I guess phone calls make me nervous. Which is a pretty sorry state of affairs when you think of it—I'm a secretary. But there you are. I just didn't know what to think," she said again. She was trying to get Mrs. Patterson to smile. Anybody in Spence could have told her what a worthless endeavor that was.

"Perhaps you don't understand the seriousness of this, Mrs. Combs. We cannot have fighting at this school." Mama looked at me again.

"No, of course not. Fighting. Definitely not." She smiled at me, and I felt my heart resume its beat. Had I been sitting there for half an hour without a heartbeat? I believe I had. "Still," Mama went on, "I'm glad it wasn't anything, you know, really awful." She whispered this last. It seemed to infuriate Mrs. Patterson.

"And exactly what do *you* call fighting, with a boy? What do *you* call a broken nose?" The control in her voice was terrifying.

"Oh, it's awful, all right. I didn't mean that," Mama said hurriedly, "and Edda, you certainly know better than to fight. I mean really. Fighting. Mmmm. But, you know," she was finishing lamely, looking then at Mrs. Patterson, "there are worse things . . . is all I meant."

"There will be a doctor's bill," Mrs. Patterson said.

"Well, we'll pay it, of course."

"I'm going to send Edda home today," Mrs. Patterson continued. "We'll consider it a one-day suspension. I expect to have from her a letter of explanation on my desk tomorrow morning and a letter of apology to Otis as well." She was looking at me.

"Listen, Mrs. Patterson," Mama said. Her tone was no longer ingratiating; it was firm. "If Edda beat up some boy in the playground, I know there was a good reason for it. She's never been in a fight before, never been in any trouble to speak of for all the years she's gone here. And you know it too."

"That's all I'm asking for, an explanation. That and an apology. Surely, you don't have a problem with that," Mrs. Patterson said, dismissing us. Mama looked for a minute like she might have a problem with it and then thought better of it.

"No. Well, good-bye then. Come on, sweetheart," she said to me, lifting me gently by one arm. She walked me out of that school with her arm on my elbow the whole time, steering me safely away.

Chapter 16

She didn't talk to me as we walked down that long hallway nor when we got in the car. Never said a word until she had pulled the car out and we were down the road a piece, headed the wrong way for home or even to pick up Jimmy at Mrs. Stumbo's, since kindergarten was only a half day. Had I thought about it, that's where I'd have assumed we were going. But no. She was just driving. Here and there. Nowhere.

"I've got an idea," she said at last. We were winding out little roads, brown earth and pine trees all around. It was February, although it could have been March, even April. There was no snow; the weather was warm. "I was thinking about going to Hazard. I want to get Annie a bottle of champagne. She has finished her collection, at last! Lucky Annie. All that work. And Edda, can you believe it, there's some gallery up in New York that wants to show it. She told me all this on the phone last night. Hey, did you know about this already? I never know what you know, my girl. So anyway, I'd thought we'd toast her good fortune in champagne. What do you think? She's going up there next week. This is real exciting for her."

I knew what she was doing. She was bathing me in words the way some mothers do with water, trying to bring my fever down. I listened to her with mild, idle interest from across the seat, looking out the window, letting trees and hills swish by. This news of Annie's was in fact news to me.

"So let's go down to Hazard, just you and me. We can get there and get back in time to pick up Jimmy at four thirty. I think I'd like to do that—what about you, sweetie?" She kept looking at me. I knew she was worried, unsure of where I was or how to proceed in getting me back. I wasn't thinking about Otis Spicer, wasn't thinking at all. Just watching out the window and listening to my mother. Coming back to life.

"I'd like to go to Hazard, Mama," I said. They were the first words out of my mouth since I'd beat up Otis, and they felt funny. I wonder how hard or easy it is to forget how to talk. It felt new again to me just then, like I hadn't done it for a long time—like oh, so that's talking.

Mama kept driving, and eventually we came out on the new road going to Hazard. In that part of eastern Kentucky, Perry County, of which Hazard is the county seat, is the closest place to buy alcohol legally. Our car, an old blue Chevy, rumbled and shook as we picked up speed on the wider highway.

"You know if you want to talk, I want to hear it, don't

you?" Mama said after a while. I said yes. She would not pry or push; that was never her way. We passed some cliff facings that were shining with icicles, bouncing sunlight. "Isn't that pretty?" Mama sighed. "You know, Edda, I don't mean to reward you for fighting, not at all. I know that *you* know that I don't approve of it. Right?"

"Yes."

"Okay. And I can see that you're pretty upset. I don't know what happened, but I know you know that I *want* to know *if* you want me to. Know, that is. Right?"

"Yes."

"And you know how I feel about fighting? Do you?"

"Yes. I know you don't like it."

"That's right. I not only don't like it, I don't approve of it either. It's the wrong way to settle differences. Do you understand that?"

"Yes."

"Do you agree?"

I thought about it then.

"Sometimes," I answered, and Mama grinned. She knew she had me back.

She slowed the car as we navigated a stretch of road that lay between two cliffs. They were man-made cliffs, blasted out when the highway was cut through but high enough to keep out the sun. There was ice on the road in that pass, even on a dry, bright February day when there had been no ice anywhere else for a week. When we climbed back up into sunlight and dry road, Mama started talking again.

"Well, what I had in mind is to stop in at that good coffee shop down there and buy us butterscotch sundaes. But I don't want you to think I'm giving you a treat for fighting in school. I'm not. It's just that"—she smiled over at me—"we don't get much private time, the two of us. And since we both have the rest of the day off, so to speak— well. That's what I was thinking about. After we get the champagne. What do you think?"

"Sounds good," I told her.

"Now, the thing is, you may have noticed that I said butterscotch. There's a reason for that. Want to know what it is?"

"What?"

"I want you to try something new, Edda. All the time with you it's chocolate, hot fudge, chocolate, chocolate. I just want you to *try* butterscotch. Okay? Just try it. What do you say?"

"What if I don't like it, Mama?"

"Hmm." She was considering. "Then I'll buy you a Hershey bar on the way out."

"It's a deal," I told her, smiling and even laughing a little. She was so good to me that day. So gentle and loving. Hershey bars even.

Her curiosity about what had provoked the fight with Otis Spicer was not greater than her profound relief that I was alive, not dead, and that although I was shaken, I was not seriously hurt, certainly not down for good. Time and talk and Hershey bars would bring me around. Her patient would live.

And so we went to Hazard and bought champagne for Annie. I tasted my first butterscotch sundae and liked it. She bought me a Hershey bar too—"for later," she said, although she let me eat it in the car on the way home. We went to pick up Jimmy at Mrs. Stumbo's, and it wasn't until our car pulled up outside her yard that I really recollected the fight. Amy came out of the house while Mama went in. I sat in the car and unrolled the window when I saw her.

"Are you okay?" she asked. She had just gotten braces; silver flashed above me.

"Yeah. I'm fine," I said.

"What happened?" she asked. "I couldn't believe my eyes, Edda. I heard you got suspended. Is that true?"

"Just one day. It's no big deal, Amy."

"No big deal." She looked at me with frank disgust. "Really."

"Is his nose really broken?" I asked. It fascinated me to think I, Edda Combs, could have broken Otis Spicer's nose.

"That's what I heard. Listen"—she was looking at me strangely; I was smiling—"see ya tomorrow. I'm freezing." A cold, fast wind had picked up; Amy's bare arms had goosebumps.

"See you tomorrow," I said.

As soon as Jimmy climbed in the car, he said, "I smell chocolate." I sat in the front seat and licked my fingers a little guiltily.

"How was school?" I asked, trying to divert him.

"Good. We had painting time," he told me, like that

was very important. Mama got in just then too and handed me a stack of his drawings. I looked through them and said *oooh* and *aah*. He grinned and grinned.

"Edda, are you famous?" he asked, as Mama started the car.

"What?" I hollered back at him over the engine noise, which was considerable. I rolled the window up.

"Are—you—famous?" he said again, very loudly, slowly.

Mama looked back at him. "Now Jimmy, where'd you hear a thing like that?"

"Bill Peyton said so. So did Amy. How come you weren't at Mrs. Stumbo's, anyway?"

"We went to Hazard," Mama told him. "And we're going to stop in at Annie's and invite her up to dinner. How's that sound? She just had some wonderful news."

"Did you go too?" Jimmy asked me, narrow-eyed, persisting still on the trail of that first whiff of chocolate.

"Uh-huh."

"Did you eat chocolate?" he asked then, zeroing in.

"Uh-huh."

"I want some too."

"Well, wait till we get home, Jimmy," Mama said. She caught my eye and winked at me.

Chapter 17

I wish I could have been more help to her. She was such good help to me that day, and then for so long after, she was such a stranger to us all, to herself, and there was nothing we could do. Nothing I could do to help her back, to help her any.

We stopped by Annie's, and Mama and Jimmy ran in. I sat on in the car, lethargic still but peaceful. They were back in a minute, and Annie came out on the porch and waved at me. I waved back, but then I started thinking. Up until I'd actually seen her, I'd forgotten that she'd been mixed up in it too. "That hippie woman." Seeing her, I remembered suddenly what Otis had said. My daddy had V.D. Got it from her. I felt again a sudden burn.

"You okay?" Mama asked, getting in the car. "You look red." I looked at her.

"Mama, what's V.D.?" I asked.

"Jimmy, put on your seatbelt," she said automatically as she started the engine. She squinted her eyes at me sideways. "Did you say V.D.?" she asked.

I nodded. "What is it?"

"Oh. Well, let's see. What's V.D.? It stands for venereal disease." I saw her glance in the rearview mirror at Jimmy. "It might be better if I explain any more about it to you later. Okay?"

"Sure, I just wanted to know. It's nothing important," I assured her.

At home Mama went upstairs to change clothes and say hello to Banker. I went up too. "Listen, Edda," she said to me in the hall as she was on her way back down to start dinner, "I think it would be a good thing for you to get those letters for Mrs. Patterson out of the way before we eat. Okay?"

"Sure," I said, hoping I sounded casual. I'd completely forgotten about them. Jimmy was upstairs too, and I kicked him out of our room. "Beat it," I told him, "vamoose. Go see Banker or go downstairs or go outside. I've got to think, Jimmy. I need privacy." One great thing about Jimmy was he understood the word privacy from the time he was two years old. He would always leave me alone when I needed it.

I got out the dictionary and looked up V.D. There were two entries, *Vd* and *V.D.* The first stood for vanadium, the chemical; it couldn't be that. And then, under it, I saw the words Mama had used, *venereal disease*. I turned the pages— "venereal, adj. ⟨from the Latin, *venereus, venus*, love⟩, 1. having to do with sexual love or intercourse. 2. transmitted by sexual intercourse with an infected person; as, syphilis

and gonorrhea are venereal diseases. 3. infected with a venereal disease. 4. for the cure of such a disease: as a venereal
remedy."

It didn't make a lot of sense to me. I had vaguely suspicioned, even on the playground, that it had something
to do with sex. But love too, apparently. A disease of love?
Of sex? I did not know what to make of it.

Dear Mrs. Patterson, I wrote in my best script. *I got in a
fight today with Otis Spicer because of something he said. It
had to do with love and sex and I don't want to go into it
word for word, if you don't mind. I realize violence is wrong
and against the rules too. Sincerely, Edda Combs.*

I didn't want to bring my father into it, and I figured
the love and sex part ought to satisfy her.

The apology to Otis didn't come out so easily.

Dear Otis, I wrote. *I'm sorry I didn't break your jaw while
I was at it.* I scratched that out. *Dear Otis, I know it's
wrong to hit people, but if you ever so much as* think *anything
about my father again, I'm going to kill you.*

I had to throw the letter away. I could only conjure threats
and more threats. My only sincere regret was that I hadn't
hurt him worse than a measly broken nose.

I went outside. It was cold by then and almost completely
dark. The porch light was on, and I swung for a while on

the swing, watching my shadow zoom up and down the plank boards. Annie drove up. "Edda, aren't you cold out here?" she asked as she passed me on her way inside. We were both blowing steam into the freezing night, but no, I didn't feel cold. Not that she'd waited for an answer.

Mama called me to come set the table. She was opening the champagne just as I went into the kitchen. "Everybody watch out!" she said, giggling. The cork popped, and she poured the bubbly liquid into two tall wine glasses. She and Annie clinked them together; both were smiling. "To my good friend," Mama said, "my dear friend, my sister, Annie Adams. A great artist."

Annie smiled even bigger and, blushing a little, said, "Oh, Frances." They drank the first sip solemnly.

"Mmm. It's good. I wonder if Banker would like some," Mama said. "I'll go see."

"Taste," Jimmy said to Annie as soon as Mama had left the room. She giggled at him.

"You little conniver. Okay. One. And I mean a sip. Got it?" Jimmy nodded and took the glass. His nose caught a bubble and he sprang back from it. Annie laughed again. "Do you want a sip, Edda?" she called over to me. I shook my head no. I was setting the table like it was something I'd never done before. It was taking an immense amount of concentration.

At dinner Annie and Mama talked excitedly about New York. "I wish I was going with you," Mama said. She remembered a lot of places up there and told Annie several times, "Go out on the Staten Island ferry." Annie had been to New York more times even than Mama, but she'd never been on that. "Listen, I know what you're thinking, it's such a touristy thing to do and all that, but so what? It's worth it. Do it, Annie. I mean it."

"I will if I have time," Annie conceded.

"No, no you don't," Mama said cheerfully. "I'm talking about *making* time, Annie. You've got to make time for things. Don't you, Edda?" she smiled at me. "Edda and I made some time for each other this afternoon, and it was really nice, wasn't it?"

I smiled at her and looked away. In a minute, I knew, if she kept up with this subject, she was going to remember that the time we'd had was made *for* us. And why.

"What did you two get into this afternoon?" Annie asked.

"Well, we went to Hazard, for one thing," Mama said, and I could tell by the way she was looking at me then, she was remembering, as I'd feared, how it had come about. "Did you get those letters written?" she asked me then, kind of low.

"I got one. The one to Mrs. Patterson," I said. "I'm sort of stuck on the other one."

"Oh." She nodded, and for a moment the gesture reminded me of Banker. "Apologies can be very hard." She looked down at her plate for a minute. "But they're important, sweetie; they really are."

"Edda's famous," Jimmy said then, as though by way of explanation to Annie.

"Is she really?" Annie asked, looking at me with an expectant grin. "And what did she do to earn fame and apology all in one day?"

Mama looked up. "Do you want to talk about it, Edda?"

I shrugged.

"She got in a fight at school," Mama said. "And Jimmy, if this is going to get around school, I want you to just ignore it, you hear?" To Annie she said, "I had a little heart attack this afternoon when the school called me at work. Thank God, it was nothing worse."

"Who'd you get in a fight with, Edda?" Annie asked. She was always asking names of people at school. She knew a lot of kids' older brothers or sisters from up at the high school.

"Otis Spicer." I said. "He's a jerk." Then, looking at Mama, I added, "Although I do know fighting is wrong."

"You got in a fight with Otis Spicer?" Annie hooted, like this was big news, a great joke. "What happened?" I didn't say anything.

"Well, we think she broke his nose," Mama said at last, very quietly.

"Whoo girl! Go get him," Annie said approvingly. "I know his father," she said to Mama, "and *he's* a jerk too." She made a face. Mama smiled a little doubtfully.

"Well, I really don't approve. We've talked about it though, haven't we, Edda?" I nodded at her and ate some food. I have no idea what. "Fighting isn't any good. She got suspended for it too, Annie, so it isn't funny. But just one day," she added. "And really, Edda, I meant to tell you this earlier—don't worry about that part. The suspension and the 'this will go on your permanent record card' stuff. I mean it. There *is* no permanent record card. Lord, I wish I'd known that when I was in school. I probably shouldn't tell you this, but I think he wouldn't mind. Your father got suspended from school too, when he was in high school, for some prank. He and a bunch of boys ran somebody's underwear up the flag pole. Did you ever?" She was clucking. "Tchk, tchk, tchk." Smiling too though, to show it didn't matter. "That part doesn't worry me one bit. But now fighting, that's worse."

"What happened?" Annie demanded of me. Mama had not asked me that question directly, would not. Annie, however, felt no hesitation. She was smiling at me, confident that she had the right to ask me anything. Suddenly, fiercely, I hated her.

Had I not hated her just then, I wouldn't have blurted it out. "He said Daddy had V.D. and that *you* gave it to him." Had I not said that, her face would not have gone pale, Mama would not have gasped, and the world might have been a different place. Just as I said it, the phone rang, making us all jump. It was Mrs. Spicer, calling to apologize for Otis—first to Mama and then to me. She said she was sorry that her boy had been so rude. They had had a little family problem, and she was sorry. It was no business of his to be spreading meanness around. That's what she said to me as I held the phone to my ear.

"It's okay, Mrs. Spicer," I said, repeating word for word what I'd heard Mama say a minute before, "Thank you." I hung up the phone. I wondered if this meant I didn't have to write that note to Otis after all.

Mama kept looking at Annie, real blankly, stupidly almost. Annie was sitting there, white as a sheet; she had started to cry. Mama said, "This is a bad joke, isn't it? Isn't it?" Nobody said a word. She looked at Jimmy and then at me and said, "You all go, please. Go." Her voice was so soft, so certain that there was no thought of arguing. We both slipped out of our chairs and left the room.

We didn't go far. Jimmy had no real idea of what was going on, but he was uneasy with the strange swift undercurrents that had swirled up all at once. I was little better but knew somehow I'd been in the center of it. We went into the living room, not talking. I looked at the picture shelves and strained to hear voices in the kitchen. Jimmy lay down on the couch.

At first the talk was so low I couldn't make any of it out. But then, as I knew somehow we would, we heard Mama screaming. Jimmy looked at me with fear in his eyes, and I went to him then, sat with him on the couch. He was sucking two fingers. At first she did not scream words, only sounds, and that made it worse. They were animal sounds, hardly human.

"*Aaaaieeee. Owwwaaa.*" I could hear Annie talking low and fast, trying to calm her down. "*No! No! No!*" Mama screamed. "I didn't know. How dare you sit there and look at me like that?" She was spitting words like bullets. *"You thought I knew? All this time? All these years? No. No. Aaagghh."*

We could hear Annie crying and mumbling, "I'm sorry, Frances. I'm so sorry. I'm sorry."

"Don't you sorry me!" Mama screamed. Her voice sounded horrible, ugly and raw. *"When I was pregnant? No.* I don't believe you. *I hate you for this, Annie Adams.* How *could* you? When I was pregnant?" And then the fury broke, and we could hear her sobbing.

Jimmy started crying too. He was whimpering, and big tears were falling down his cheeks. Suddenly, I wanted to get away. "Come on," I told him. "Let's go upstairs." He shook his head and drew away from me when I tugged at his arm. I knew what he was doing; how often had I done it myself? But I no longer felt able to stand guard. There was nothing left I wanted to know, and there was no way to protect her, nothing we could do to ease her pain. I wanted to run.

"No, you may not say good-bye." Mama was screaming again but choking on the words, on tears. *"Haven't you done them harm enough? I said get out and I mean now. Damn you. Now."* Something slammed on something else. Nothing broke. And then we heard Annie, crying still and mumbling, leaving through the back door.

"Jimmy, please," I whispered. "Let's go upstairs." He buried his head in the pillow on the couch and cried harder. Then he was up and running, into the kitchen, to Mama.

I shut my eyes and waited. I could hear them both in there, crying together. I imagined he was on her lap, her head in his curls, his face on her shoulder. I went upstairs.

"Banker?" I tapped on his door.

"Yes. Oh, Edda, come in. Sounds like some kind of trouble down there. Are you all right?" He was in his chair, and although I was a big girl now, too big really to squeeze in with him, I did. Somehow he made room for me.

"Something terrible's happened," I told him. "I'm not sure what it is, but Mama's in a bad way, Banker. A real bad way. Worse than ever." I was trying to distinguish the badness of this, make him see it.

"I heard some noise," he said.

"Well, see, it started at school today, with me." And I told him, told him all I knew, right down to V.D. and Mrs. Spicer's phone call. And then I was crying too, and he was patting my hair and saying, "No, no, darling, this is not your doing."

Chapter 18

But it *was* my doing, my fault. I could not let Banker console me. That night, when Mama brought Jimmy to bed, I pretended to be asleep, a ruse she saw right through. She sat on the side of my bed, waiting, and I finally gave it up and opened my eyes. She looked so strange, wild even, her eyes red and puffy. But there was something missing from her face. Her mouth. Her lips were drawn in, simply gone. Only a stretched white line remained.

"Mama, I'm sorry," I said. Partly I was talking out of terror; her odd looks and her silence were scaring me. Also, I felt truly that I had brought this on, whatever it was.

"I'm sorry too, Edda," she answered in a hoarse, low tone. I couldn't think of anything else to say, and I could see she was beyond helping me with words of her own. After a while she looked back over at Jimmy and got up, turned out the light, and left.

We ate breakfast in almost perfect silence the next morning. Neither Jimmy nor I had either the courage or the heart to make small talk to a woman with no lips. When we drove by Annie's house, Mama looked straight ahead. At school, before he climbed out of the car, Jimmy leaned up and whispered into her neck, "I love you, Mama." She said, "I love you too, Jimmy," flatly, nothing else. I was standing on the pavement by then, holding the door for him. I wanted to say, "Me too, Mama, I love you too," but I couldn't. I wanted her to say, "I love you too, Edda," but she didn't. We went up the steps.

My homeroom teacher sent me to the office; I had to have a note from Mrs. Patterson before she'd let me back in class. Yesterday, when I'd been sitting in the front seat of the car with the window rolled down, talking to Amy, I'd felt like a "dangerous character" and enjoyed it. Today I was still being treated like one, but I felt so far from that role, so fundamentally different from that wild and crazy Edda Combs who beat up Otis Spicer that it seemed absurd.

I had to wait to see Mrs. Patterson. I sat in the front office, looking at the secretary, who was looking at me. I could see kids passing in the hall, feel their eyes on me, hear the high pitch of excitement in their whispers as they walked on. "Edda Combs. I hear it's broke good, in two places. Her father's dead." My father being dead had remained an important part of my identity at Spence. Now I was also the *girl* who beat up Otis Spicer.

Mrs. Patterson's door opened and she stood there looking at me. My stomach tightened. I'd forgotten the letter, come off to school without it. How could I have done that?

"I wrote it," I said, "but I forgot it, Mrs. Patterson. That's the truth."

150·

"As I recall, I asked you for two letters. Did you—forget—both of them?" Very sarcastic.

"Well, no, ma'am."

"Well, I'm waiting."

"Well, actually, you see, I only wrote the one." How could I tell her about Mrs. Spicer's phone call?

"Which 'one' exactly did you see fit to write?"

"The one to you."

"I beg your pardon?"

"The one to you," I said louder. "I'll bring it tomorrow, I promise. I'm sorry."

"I'll have to call your mother."

"What? No, you can't do that."

"I beg your pardon?"

"I mean, she just got to work herself. She might not even be there. Yet."

"Nevertheless, Edda, you were suspended. I cannot allow you back into school without the required reparations. Do you know what reparations are?"

"Yes, ma'am. No, ma'am. The letters?"

"Amends. Repairs. Apparently, neither you nor your mother have been sufficiently impressed with the seriousness of this situation. I simply will not stand for fighting in school. The fact that you are a girl makes it distasteful as well."

"Oh, but we do understand. My mother talked to me a long time yesterday about how bad it was to fight. I know I shouldn't have done it. I'm sorry. I'm sorry."

I apologized profusely that morning. I would go on apol-

ogizing for years. For anything. You're not feeling well?
I'm sorry. It's raining? I'm sorry. I'm sorry, Mrs. Patterson;
I'm sorry, Mama; I'm sorry, everybody. Everybody but Otis
Spicer. I still hated him. I lied through my teeth that I was
sorry about hitting him, but for the rest of it I really was
sorry.

She decided to call Mama anyway, to "impress upon her
the gravity of the situation and her responsibilities" as my
mother. I sat there with a terrible knot in my stomach as
Mrs. Patterson dialed the number, as they talked. They
didn't talk long.

Again I sat out in the front office waiting for Mama.
Again I heard her step before I saw her, a much different
step than the day before. She glanced at me briefly when
she entered the office—like I was a stranger or somebody
else's kid.

"I'm sorry, Mama," I whispered.

"That's all right, Edda." A clipped, businesslike, unfamiliar version of herself. "You can stay right there," she
said to me. "This doesn't concern you."

"I beg to differ with you, Mrs. Combs," Mrs. Patterson
said.

"Please step into your office and shut the door," Mama
said firmly, stepping in there herself.

I don't know what they said. The secretary and I exchanged glances, both of us frankly eavesdropping. But
there was nothing to hear but the rise and fall of their voices.
When they came out, Mama looked at me and said, "You
can go back to class now."

"I need a note," I whispered.

"She needs a note," she reported to Mrs. Patterson in that flat voice. And to my utter amazement Mrs. Patterson bent down and wrote me a pass.

Mama and I left the office together. Although her limp was more pronounced than usual, she was walking quickly; I almost had to run to keep up with her. Just before she reached the door, before I had to turn down the hall to my class, she stopped and spoke to me. "Listen, Edda. Keep your head up and don't take flak from anybody. Not today and not ever. Just keep your head up. You hear me?" I nodded. "Okay. I love you. See you later."

"Mama," I called as she was pushing open those big front doors. She stopped and the sun was bright overhead; it poured into the hall. "I love you too." I was afraid suddenly that I would cry, which to me would have been a far worse thing to do in school than beat up Otis Spicer.

"I know that, Edda. Good-bye." She went through the door, and it slammed darkly shut.

It was the deadness in her voice that was so frightening. When she'd been sad, I knew we could cheer her up or at least make her smile; when she was angry, we always knew it would pass. But this, this was unlike anything I'd ever heard from her before—past sad, past angry, past anything she'd ever been.

Otis Spicer looked terrible. He had big black and purple patches on his nose and cheeks, under his eyes. His face was swollen out of proportion. I found out later that I hadn't been responsible for it all, that his father had beat him up too, but at first I was awed by the power that was evidently mine. He was sullen and angry; I was shaken and afraid. We exchanged one brief, ugly look.

At recess Charlie found me. I was alone, standing there. "Hey, Edda, want to fight?" he asked, sparring, grinning at me.

"Not you too," I groaned. I was very tired already, after half a day, of that joke.

"Nah. I'm only kidding. Are you okay?" He sincerely was asking, wanted to know.

"Yeah. I'm fine, just fine." I looked at him and smiled and then, to my horror, realized there were tears standing in my eyes. I looked away and dug furiously at them with my fist. Charlie, to his credit, looked away and kicked at the dirt.

He took a lot of teasing about being my friend. We both did to some extent, but he got the brunt of it after my little "incident" with Otis. Other kids said things like "Your girlfriend going to protect you?" or "You better do what*ever* she says, Charlie." He would look sad when people talked that way, but he never punched anybody out over it. For a while, that's what I wanted him to do, what I wanted to do myself. But neither one of us had the temperament or the stamina to be fighters; it's an exhausting reputation to maintain. Instead, I became more of what I'd been already, a loner. And Charlie, who was not a loner, who fit in well with almost everyone, wore the tag of being my friend like a tattoo. It was just one of those things about him—he liked Edda Combs. Since it was Charlie, even something as aberrant as that could be accepted.

That afternoon after school Mrs. Stumbo beckoned me upstairs to her bedroom. Bobby McIntosh, the baby, was taking a nap in there, so all the lights were out and the curtains drawn. "Edda," she whispered to me, "I just want to say something to you." I looked at her expectantly. It was so odd to be alone with her in the dark. "Your daddy was a fine man, and I think the world of your mother. I want you to know that. Okay?" I nodded. "That's all," she hissed, and I could see her white teeth glowing at me. I waited anyway, and sure enough there was more. "Tommy Spicer's wife caught him with his pants down with that art teacher woman. He's upset and trying to spread it around, Edda. You should have never been caught in the middle of this trash in the first place. Pay it no mind. Your daddy was a good man, remember that."

"Yes ma'am, I will," I whispered back. I could see the dim reflection of both of us in the huge mirror that stood over the dresser.

"I'm praying for your mother, Edda. Our whole group is. I know Jesus will take care of this. So don't you worry."

"What group?" I asked. It alarmed me to think of a "whole group" praying for Mama. What for?

"Our Wednesday night prayer group. The Lord is very good to us. Just last week He moved among us and healed Callie Evers' eye infection. Healed it, just like that. Nothing is too much to ask the Lord, Edda. You remember that."

"Yes ma'am."

When we emerged from that dark room, back into the noisy light of the house, I looked at Mrs. Stumbo again. Her blond hair was sprayed and set in place as always. There was a stiffness to it that I frankly admired. No matter what she did, it stayed in place, flipped up just the slightest bit in the back, smooth around her face. I tried to imagine her praying. I wanted to see what her eyes looked like closed; open they were sparkly green with green eyeshadow on the lids, her lashes black and long and sticky with mascara.

I didn't mention to Mama that she was being prayed for. Somehow, I didn't think she would appreciate knowing that, and besides, there was no way to make conversation with her. Jimmy and I tiptoed around her for days, weeks, careful to be quiet, to be good. She rarely spoke to us at all, and when she did it was only to issue terse orders. "Bed." "Dinner." "Get in the car." "Feed the cat." "Take a bath." I don't think she talked to Banker at all. The pinched white line which was all that remained of her mouth opened only when necessary, clamming shut again almost immediately.

One day a postcard came in the mail. It was a picture of the Statue of Liberty, all lit up at night. Mama glanced at it and tore it in two. After she'd gone upstairs, I fished it out of the wastebasket and pieced it together.

Frances, Annie wrote in her neat, almost calligraphic script. *You were right about the ferry. Have you never been wrong? Forgive me. Please. I love you. Annie.*

A few weeks later I saw lights on at Annie's house and I knew she was back from New York. One day I heard Mama answer the phone, heard her say in that tone cold as death, "I told you to leave us alone and I meant it. Don't call again." To my knowledge, Annie never did.

Chapter 19

Mama wrapped herself in rage, and the pure cold edge of it held her erect, kept her going. But it's also what finally broke her. It started out with her teeth. One morning she awoke in pain, to find she had broken a tooth in her sleep. She went, right away, to the dentist, who told her she was clenching her jaw as she slept, grinding her teeth. He fitted her with a piece of clear plastic called a "night guard" or a "bite guard." I never could get it straight. In the mornings, if I'd see her before she got up, there was a rim of plastic on her upper teeth. Her words came out spongy and indistinct until she removed it. In some weird way it was a relief to know she couldn't bite us when she had it in. Not that she ever bit us, bit anybody that I'd ever heard of, but the anger in her mouth, in her jaw, was tangible. And she was such a stranger to us—we thought she might be capable of anything.

She began to suffer headaches too that spring, bad ones. Sometimes she'd wake up with them and couldn't get out of bed. Those mornings I'd fix breakfast: cereal and milk or nothing. Jimmy and I would just eat bread, standing up. Then we'd walk out Cauley's Creek to catch the school bus at the store, leaving Mama asleep or half awake in her dark room. Banker got no coffee those mornings unless he made it himself, which I doubt he did.

One morning she threw up. She had a headache but not too bad, she said. She was up and fixing breakfast, getting ready for work, when she bolted upstairs to the bathroom, and we heard her up there retching. After a long time she called down to me, and I went up. She was sitting on the bathroom floor, her long black hair stringy, her pale face even paler. She looked like a witch but a very sick one.

"I need help, Edda," she said in a voice so low and thick I could barely hear her. "Help me up," she said. I took her arm and pulled. Her head tumbled forward, and for a moment I was afraid it might actually tumble off, that she might literally fall apart. "I'm so dizzy," she moaned, pushing herself up, using the toilet seat for leverage. Mama swayed and stumbled as I helped her back to her room, to her bed, which she lay on, fully dressed, face down. "Turn off the light. Take care of Jimmy. Catch the bus." She said all that to her pillow, but I obeyed.

Jimmy liked the bus, probably because we only rode it now and then. He liked to go into the store where we waited, and talk with the men who were always gathered there, near the front by the pickled bologna and the crackers. Even in the morning there were men there. They would chat with Jimmy, and he would chat back—easy, open small talk for which he had a gift. In the afternoons we'd stop in there and pick up Banker's papers. People would ask after Mama, and Jimmy would say, "She's fine," like it was true. I said the same thing, but it never came out so convincing. On the bus he smiled at everybody, said "Hey" a million times in greeting to kids that I, who had gone to school much longer, barely recognized.

One day I told Amy about my mother throwing up. "Is she pregnant?" Amy asked.

"I doubt that," I said. "It takes two, you know."

"I know, but did *you* know that throwing up was one of the symptoms?"

"Yeah, I know that." We were outdoing one another with our vast knowledge of the female reproductive system. "She threw up when she was pregnant with Jimmy. This is different. She *can't* be pregnant, Amy. I know that much."

"Well, you never know, Edda." She was smiling at me with smug sophistication.

"Oh yes, I do," I said angrily. "I know about sex, more than you. I know about V.D." I hadn't meant to say that. I never talked about V.D. Mama had never mentioned it again, and I certainly didn't bring it up.

"What is that, anyway?" Amy asked.

"Oh," I said breezily, "it's a disease of love."

"Really? What happens?" Amy asked.

"Well, I'm not sure. But you get sick somehow." I was in territory now that I knew next to nothing about. "You see, it comes from Venus—you know, the goddess of love?"

Charlie had showed me a book called *Word Origins*, and we were both interested in it. "That's what it stands for, Venus."

Amy giggled. "It sound like youknowwhat."

I had to think a minute before I caught the joke. Venus—penis. "Well, it's nothing like that. It so happens Venus was the Roman goddess of love. War too, I think."

"Venus Disease?" Amy asked. "Do you think that's what your mother has? I mean if she's not pregnant?"

"What, V.D.? Nah, she couldn't have that." But I wondered. What did she have?

I don't mean to give the impression that my mother took to her bed and stayed there. She did not. Most of the time she was up and about, silent, unsmiling, but up. She was up the day we found Mrs. Roosevelt dead over in a patch of grass beyond the coal shed. Jimmy was playing over there, I was reading on the front porch swing, and Mama was hanging up laundry. I heard him yell and start to cry. He was on his knees in the grass, calling to Mama and crying. She and I both went over.

Mrs. Roosevelt was lying stiff as a board; her eyes were wide open, so was her mouth. The only things moving on her were a few wisps of her long gray-and-white fur. Jimmy was running his hands through it. Mama looked and then froze. Her eyes widened as she stared. Suddenly, she grabbed Jimmy's arm, grabbed him hard, and yanked him up, pulling him away from the cat. "Come wash your hands. Quick." As she jerked him into the house, she said to me, "Don't touch her, Edda." I didn't. I just stood there looking at her. Her death gape. She died in agony, but we never did figure out how. Poison is what Mama said. Banker disagreed. Who would poison Mrs. Roosevelt? She hardly ever went anywhere; she stayed around our place.

Mama dug her grave that afternoon. The earth was dry and full of rocks. I helped her with it some but couldn't get much purchase on the shovel. When it was done, she put on gloves and wrapped Mrs. Roosevelt in a clean towel. Jimmy and I stood by. "I commend this dear cat to God," she said, staring hard, straight down at the open hole.

"Amen," I said. Jimmy started to cry again.

"And if this was done by human hands," Mama continued, looking up, her voice breaking clear and sharp in the evening air, "may that one suffer the same."

A deep, deep chill ran through my bones. I was glad I'd said amen before she'd said her curse.

After that a lot of things happened in a row, real fast, none of them good. A tree limb blew down in the middle of a storm one night and broke two windows in the front of the house. It looked like we'd been hit by vandals. The water pipes in the kitchen burst again. Henry John was long gone, and it was a week or more before Mama could find anyone to fix them. We hauled water, and she threw her back out doing it. Not only did she limp, she was bent up, in pain. Her left arm went numb, right down to the fingers. She couldn't type. Mr. Robinson told her about a chiropractor over in Wise County, Virginia. He helped her some, but she was still all crooked. Off.

She took to dropping things. Maybe it was the numbness in her hand; maybe it was more than that. All she ever dropped, that broke, were pieces of china, glasses, and fine, fancy dishes—"special things" she and Daddy had been given for wedding presents. I knew which they were because so often she had pointed them out to me, let me hold them, and told me who had given them what. Now they were breaking, one after another. At dinner one night, when she was carrying a dish of chicken to the table, she dropped it. The dish, one of those special ones, shattered; chicken and gravy flew everywhere. I jumped up to help, but Mama wasn't moving, just standing there in the midst of it all. She was so quiet that Jimmy and I stayed quiet too. Then she said, very calmly, conversationally almost, "Ed, I quit. It's over. I've had it."

The hairs on the back on my neck stood up. I almost looked around to see if he was there. Jimmy did. It was like that, like he was standing right there and she was talking to him. Like he might answer back.

But of course he didn't. Daddy was dead and would answer no more. Instead, Mama picked up the mess, saying nothing. She cleaned off her shirt where it was spattered with grease and mopped up the floor. She put the chicken in another bowl and brought it to the table where we sat watching. "Eat it anyway," she said. We did.

"Children," she said after a while, "I've come to a decision." We both looked up. She was not eating, just sitting there. "I'm going to divorce your father." No one said a word. I stared at her and thought, She's lost her mind. My mother is crazy. It's not V.D. It's insanity.

Jimmy smiled at her. This was, after all, more words than she'd strung together all at one time in weeks. "Okay," he said pleasantly, encouraging her. She smiled at him, a vacant curve on the tight line of her mouth.

"No," I said furiously, "No, it's not okay." I started crying. "Mama, Mama, it's not okay. No."

"Edda," she said, looking straight at me, deep into me, "I know this is hard for you to accept."

"Mama, he's dead," I cried. Had she forgotten?

"That has nothing to do with it. It's beside the point entirely."

"Well it's not to *me*," I yelled and ran off to my room, away from her and her crazy eyes, her crazy voice, her crazy ideas.

I lay on my bed and cried for a long time. I remembered how she'd talked to Daddy in the kitchen, like he was there, and I wished, even though I might have to be crazy to do it, that I could talk to him too. That he would talk to me, talk to her, stop her, help her, help me.

I knew about divorce. There were plenty of kids at school whose parents got divorced. There were rumors that spring that Otis Spicer's parents were going to. Charlie had a cousin who saw his father only on the weekends. And only sometimes. All of a sudden I started laughing, thinking that if

Mama got divorced from Daddy, maybe it would mean I could see him on the weekends. It wasn't fun laughing, and soon my stomach started hurting. Maybe I'm crazy after all, I thought, but I couldn't stop laughing no matter what.

And then I thought: I hate her. I hate Mama for being crazy. I hate her for wanting to divorce Daddy. I hate her. And more. I hate Daddy too. I hate him for being dead. And if he did have V.D. with Annie, I hate him for that too. I hate them both.

It was the first time I ever really thought such a thing, thought it clearly and knew it for certain. It shocked me enough to stop me laughing. Instead I lay there, catching my breath. I heard Mama coming up the steps and got up, pretending to do some homework. She stood in the doorway of my room and said, "Do you want to talk?" I shook my head no. She just kept standing there, looking at me. Finally she went into her room and shut the door.

I went to Banker. He was cutting up newspapers, using his big silver scissors. I didn't even wait for him to say, "Come in," just barged in on him.

"Banker, I've got to talk to you," I said.

"I can see that," he answered me mildly. "What's up?"

"I think . . ." I paused. How could I explain this? "Banker, I think Mama's . . . uh . . ."

He waited. I waited; nothing came to me. "You're worried about Frances?" he offered.

"You could say that." You could say that if you didn't know that here stood a girl who hated her mother.

"She's had a very hard time here lately," Banker said.

"I know that, but this is more. More than a hard time, I mean."

"Tell me then."

"Do you know what divorce is?" Banker, for all his knowledge, had huge gaps. I was just checking to see if this was one of them.

"Yes, I'm familiar with it," he said, smiling at me gently. "What about it? Don't tell me that you and that Henson boy are having problems?"

"Banker, I'm trying to talk to you serious. Besides," I said, blushing, "we're not even that kind of—of—you know, friends."

"I'm sorry, Edda. I can see you're in no mood for an old man's feeble jokes. What about divorce?"

"Mama said, down in the kitchen, at dinner . . . Mama said she was—was going to . . . to . . . ." I started crying again. Saying the words was too much.

"What, Edda?" Banker asked very gently, reaching his old wrinkled white hand out for me. But I could not say it, could not go on.

Just then, like a shot in the back, Mama's hard, cold voice answered for me, "I'm going to divorce Ed, Banker. That's what she's trying to tell you."

Chapter 20

Banker, whom I had rarely ever seen even ruffled, raised his bushy white eyebrows in dismay, or at least surprise. I thought: I knew it, she *is* crazy. Now even Banker can tell. But all he said was, "Won't you come in?"

Mama sat in the chair by his desk, that long rough-hewn table of his. She seemed calm and poised. She met his eyes without flinching or tears. "Banker, Edda"—she nodded at me—"I know this is hard. But it's something I've set my mind on. I *must* do it. Must. Edda, I think, is too young to understand that, but you, Banker, can you?"

"I know there are things we feel compelled to do from time to time. Even things that are awkward or difficult. But Frances, it seems a bit unfair to be divorcing Ed when he can't be here to contest it, to defend himself."

"He couldn't even contest it if he were alive," Mama said. "He could hold it up, but he couldn't stop me. Not in this state, not even here in Kentucky could he do that. Not anymore."

Banker nodded. "Yes, they passed that bill at the last general assembly if I remember correctly."

"Yes, they did, Banker. And I'm going to divorce him. Period." It disturbed me that Banker was addressing the legality of it rather than the insanity. What was wrong?

"It still doesn't seem quite fair," Banker continued.

"Fair?" Mama spat out the word like it had a bad taste. "Was it fair of Ed to have an affair with my best friend while I was pregnant? Was that fair?" Her voice was rising. "Was it fair that he slept with that—that woman, that whore who had herpes, and then slept with me? Is that fair? Was it fair that he and Annie could have killed the baby that way? Was that fair? Is that what you would have said if Jimmy had died? Too bad, it's not fair? I'll give you fair." She was sitting far forward in the chair, glaring at Banker, who returned her fury with a look of infinite watery-blue pity.

"So that's how it was," he said.

"Yes," she shouted, "that's how it was. The fact that I didn't catch it, that Jimmy isn't blind or dead or worse is the stroke of purest luck. Luck, Banker. *Is that fair?*"

Banker sighed. "Or the grace of God, Frances. It could have been the Goddamned grace of God."

Mama giggled. What a strange sound it was. "Yes," she said then very softly, "it could have been the grace of God. You've got a point." She looked at him and went on. "Whatever it was, luck or grace or something else entirely, I want no part of it. I want a divorce." For a while the room was still. I could hear the TV on downstairs and knew Jimmy was there, watching it.

"Death isn't good enough for you?" Banker asked gently. The phrase gave me chills.

"No, it isn't. And it's no excuse, either. I've been faithful to him through death, past death. He couldn't even do the same for me for a few lousy weeks while I was sick, while my leg was broken and we thought I was losing the baby. For God's sake." She started crying. For all those weeks when she'd been so angry there had been not a tear.

"He cheated on me, Banker, do you see that? Cheated on me and on Jimmy and even on Edda." I gave her a sharp look; I did not want my name dragged into this. She met my eyes but went on. "He lied to us. I can't tolerate a liar."

"Everybody lies, Frances. Now, surely you know that."

"No, I do *not* know that, Banker. I will not accept it. The man I married was not a liar. Why, the man I married, he was—he was—the most wonderful man in the whole world." She was brushing tears away, talking through them. "He was a man who *cared* about things, cared about people, Banker; he cared about me. He was the first one in my life . . ." She was crying then too hard to finish.

"I know he did, Frances. He loved you well. As well as he was able. I'm sure of that."

"But it wasn't well enough," Mama sobbed. "How could he do this to me? How could he?"

Banker shook his head. "That's something we can't know. I wonder if Ed were alive, would it help any, if we would know even then. Perhaps *he* didn't know. We all do things wrong. Things we feel ashamed of."

"Yes. Yes, I know that. I'm not saying I'm perfect." She laughed in the middle of her tears, laughed hard. It sounded like the laugh I had laughed not an hour earlier—hard, false. "He made a fool of me—him and Annie. All those years, all those years. It makes everything false, Banker, can't you see that?" She made a motion then with her hands, as though she was shaking off water. "Ugh, ugh," she said, still shaking her hands, holding them away from her as though they were filthy. "All my memories, Banker, they're ruined." This last was a wail, and for a long time she sat with her head in her hands, crying.

Even I, the girl who hated her mother, felt pity.

When she calmed down, when she was able again to catch her breath, she addressed me. "Edda, I need you to know something."

I nodded to show I was listening.

"Divorcing Ed, divorcing your daddy, your papa, it doesn't mean that I don't love him anymore. I will always love that man. I know that you will too. I know it. It means that I can't stay married any longer. That I won't put up with it. Not with adultery. Never. I cannot. Will not. I refuse it. And I have that right, as his wife." She looked at me to see, I think, if I was following her.

"People whose parents get divorced"—she shook her head—"the parents, I mean. They go on loving their children, no matter what. He's still your father. Nothing could change that. Nor should it. He was a very good father. To you. But he was a lousy husband, Edda. Lousy. I would never have done such a thing to him, and that he did it with Annie of all people . . ." Again she shook her head. "I don't expect you to understand all of this. Just this. I love your daddy, Edda, always will, but I will not be his wife. Nevermore."

I could not speak to her just then, but I hope it showed in my eyes that even if I hated her, I loved her too.

Banker sighed. Mama smiled at him. "Are you sad?" she asked.

"Yes, I really am."

"So am I, Banker. So am I. But I feel better too, getting it settled. Finishing up."

"Are you really going to divorce him, Frances? There's just so much in my—what would you call it?—background, I suppose, that thinks there must be another way."

"I know. My background is not so different. But I don't see any other way." She was now the gentle one.

We sat again in silence. "What's herpes?" I asked.

"It's a form of venereal disease," Mama said as though she had been expecting this.

"V.D.?"

"Yes. And if you catch it when you're pregnant, and the baby catches it too—well, it can be very bad. Herpes can be bad in any case. It's something Annie has, Edda. You mustn't speak of it outside of here."

"Did she give it to Daddy? Like Otis said?"

Mama looked puzzled for a moment. Then, "No, she didn't. Otis was wrong. But it was only by the—the"— she looked at Banker and smiled—"the grace of God that she didn't. I understand she did give it to Otis's father, and that he, Mr. Spicer, gave it to his wife. But Edda, seriously—not a word of this at school. It's important."

"Okay. I understand." In fact there was much I did not understand, but I could see that she was trusting me, needing me even. I could see too that somehow she was back. *This* woman was not crazy.

Mama left to go downstairs. Banker and I sat on a while together. "You're still a little girl to be carrying such a big load," he said to me.

"Banker, I am *not* a little girl."

"Well. Still."

"Banker, if you'd ever stand up, you'd find I'm probably taller than you," I bragged. I was trying to get him to smile. He looked very very old just then, and sad.

"That's not what I mean, Edda."

"I know."

Mama divorced Daddy that following Saturday afternoon. She told me she was going up to see him in the graveyard, and that I should watch Jimmy. I don't know what she said to him or exactly how she did it, but when she came back, she was peaceful. More so, anyway. After that she smiled sometimes and cried again the way she used to. Her mouth was never quite the same, but part of it came back. She didn't talk a lot, but some. She was better. I was better too. Hating both of my parents that night had helped me. In some way it negated the divorce. I had wed them ever after, joined them for eternity in my private book of fools.

That August Mama found a dead rat in the kitchen drawer. She'd pulled it open at breakfast, looking for forks and spoons, and there it was. A huge black creek rat. Thank God, it was dead. Mama screamed, grabbed me, grabbed Jimmy, ran us all into the living room, and jumped on the couch, pulling us up too. I'd seen that rat, and it was big. We'd had trouble with them all summer, and without Mrs. Roosevelt there for protection we too had resorted to poison. This one had crawled up in our silverware drawer to die.

When she had caught her breath, Mama started laughing. When she quit that, she said, "Okay, guys, enough of this. I've had it up to here with Cauley's Creek. We're moving. Why not? There's nothing in the Bible says you *have* to grow up in eastern Kentucky. I know there's plenty of people will say I'm wrong, but I say—let's get the hell out of here!"

And so we moved. Four years after Daddy died, a few months after their divorce, and only three weeks before school started back, we moved to Lexington. Mr. Robinson gave Mama a bottle of perfume and wished her well. She gave it to me, said it was "too young" for her. I never knew just how to say good-bye to Charlie, to Amy, to any of them. I did the best I could. Mrs. Stumbo cried and hugged me, hugged Jimmy, hugged Mama too, and said, "God bless you. We'll pray for you."

Mama said, "Thanks."

Of course we never did say good-bye to Annie. Even on that last drive down the creek, when we were packed and really going for good, Mama turned her face away from that side of the road when we passed her house.

Chapter 21

Lexington is not a big city, but it felt like that to us. We moved into a little house in a section of town that was close to the University of Kentucky. Mama had it in her mind to go back to school and get her degree in nursing. I was too old to tell her no (not that it would have done any good) and way too old to admit that the idea of her working in a hospital still scared me. But that degree was four years off; she worked as a secretary until she was able to finish it, so there wasn't any immediate concern.

The house we lived in when we first moved there was called The Living End. The landlord was a lawyer in town. When he told Mama the house's name she frowned and worked her mouth. Then she said, not really to anyone in particular, "I was hoping we could avoid this, but perhaps we aren't meant to avoid anything. We're in for it all." Banker, who was standing there, said, "Now, Frances," and the landlord looked at Mama like: Who is this lady? But she smiled at him, and they talked, and eventually she said, "How much?" The landlord's name was Mr. Ecston, but everyone I ever heard speak to him called him Mr. X, except his wife, who called him merely X.

Mr. X was in his early thirties, I guess about Mama's age. He had a full beard, so blond it looked white. Beards were something I hadn't seen much of, except on very old men of the mountains and Mr. X was not one of those. He talked in a rapid soft voice that was punctuated at uneven intervals with the accent of some unknown (at least to me) country. We saw him once a month, rarely more, when we walked up to his house with the rent. He lived directly up the street from us with his wife, two babies, and two husky dogs.

Mr. X kept a ledger showing where every "dollar and dime" went. He used that expression on me several times. It was a big, blue, flat, leatherbound book, the first of its kind that I'd ever seen. He kept it on a table in his study with an old-fashioned lamp shining on it. Mr. X was very serious about money. He gave Mama a receipt every month for our rent; he gave her receipts every time she paid him anything at all. The first time he tore that yellow paper from its pad and handed it to her, she turned to me in confusion with her eyebrows up, and said very cool, as though we did this all the time, said in a voice dry as sand, "Here, Edda. File this for us, will you?" Thus, I was elected the family bookkeeper. I, twelve years old and terrible at math. That first time she did it I was too surprised to say anything. I just took the paper from him, folded it up as neatly as I could, and slid it into my pocket as though this was a perfectly normal procedure.

"Mama," I asked her, when we were outside, walking back down the street to our house, "What do you want me to do with that receipt?"

"There, you see? You're a natural, Edda," she said, swinging her arm around my back. "I couldn't have remembered what that was called for the life of me. Do whatever you want to with it. I don't want it." And she didn't.

She could remember all kinds of medical terms; she'd recite them to us before a test. Latin—you name it. But if it had to do with business, with money of any kind, she couldn't remember the slightest thing about it. So I took it over, and over time I got pretty good at it. She never did. She'd say, "I just don't have a head for finances," as if this was regrettable, but I believe she was secretly proud of it.

Banker might have seemed the natural choice in our family to do bookkeeping; after all, he already kept records of things. But he didn't want to fool with money either. When his checks came in, like clockwork every month, he immediately handed them over to Mama, who in time came to hand them quickly, gratefully over to me.

I learned that we were chronically short of money. Maybe we always had been, but now I was aware of it, and at times it worried me severely. She said that the rent we paid in Lexington was three times what we paid on Cauley's Creek but it couldn't be avoided. Pay any less and we were likely to end up with rats in the silverware drawer again. Mama took a part-time job as a typist for a public health clinic, and depending on which semester it was, she sometimes

·177

had a small stipend from the university to buy books. We received a small check from the government for Daddy's veteran's benefits and another from the state for his death. Banker drew a little social security, and that was it. All written out, it sounds like more than it was. Every month I faced the bills, which seemed large, and tried to patch together these small checks, to make them cover. It didn't always work. Mama never complained about it or about my bookkeeping, even when it didn't come out right. When I'd worry about it out loud, she'd say, "We live like kings and queens, Edda. Kings and queens." Did she really believe that? Well, I'll admit that we never went hungry.

Why, of all places, did we move to Lexington? Why not Kansas City or New York or any other town? Why not the beach since she loved that so well? For one thing, Banker didn't want to go far. Having been born in Kentucky, having lived out all his life there, he said he would like to go on living there till he died. Mama said she didn't want to go too far either, said she hadn't the energy for anything stranger.

And The Living End was strange enough for her. Possibly it'd be strange enough for anyone. It was once a large house that had been divided in two. We lived in the bigger part of it and had a living room, kitchen, bathroom, small bedroom downstairs (Banker's room), and three small bedrooms upstairs. Really, I'm stretching it to say it had three bedrooms upstairs. It had two rooms and a big closet that served as Jimmy's room. He hardly ever complained about it, even after he grew so much and kept bumping his head on the ceiling. I was very happy to have a room of my own at long last.

Next door to us lived an assortment of people who came and went in what, at least in memory, seems no particular order: a gun-toting electrician who would go on rages in the middle of the night and shoot cats in the alley (he was eventually arrested), a woman whose husband or ex-husband came around regularly and beat her (Mama would call the police, and we'd sit in silence waiting for them to get there), an artist who painted a mural on the bathroom wall as a return favor for the dinners Mama fed him, a man who kept a tarantula in a cage, said it was his pet (that guy mostly drank beer and lay around the house). There were lots of them, more than I can even remember. Most of them were old friends of Mr. X's who'd fallen on hard times. The Living End was known as some sort of haven. Our neighbors came and went.

We stayed on. Mr. X let us get behind on our heating bills in the winter, partly because, I think, he knew we weren't going anywhere. By the standards of The Living End we were stable. We knew our neighbors because we shared the back hallway with them, because the house wasn't really very big and the walls were thin, and because somehow, out of all those people, none of them ever had a phone. They were always coming over to borrow ours, so we knew them.

The house fronted on a busy main street. The hardest

thing for me was getting used to the noise. I'd never thought about Cauley's Creek being quiet, but it was, compared to that. All night long there were trucks going by or tires squealing. There were boys yelling from car windows and ladies laughing, suddenly, in the middle of the night.

I was lonely. I guess I had high hopes about being in a new place and starting over. I was in the seventh grade, and in Lexington, the seventh, eighth, and ninth grades were a separate school, junior high. In Spence there was one elementary school for kindergarten through eighth grade and one high school, grades nine through twelve. I thought that here, in a new place, a place so big nobody cared who anybody else was related to, I would be known for who I truly was, the "I" I could sense inside me, straining to be born. I was twelve years old, had just got my period (got it, actually, in the car on the trip up to Lexington) and thought my life was about to begin. Surely some part of it did, but it was a slow start. At a place as big as Chandler Junior High, I found that, whoever I was or wasn't, nobody cared anyway.

School started almost immediately after we moved. On my first day, before I left the house, Mama said, "Edda, I just don't want you to do drugs or have sex until you get out of high school, okay?"

"Mama," I said in my most thoroughly disgusted voice, "don't be ridiculous."

"Well, this is a different place than what you're used to. Don't try to tell me there won't be kids into drugs; I know there are. And about sex, well, I just want you to wait."

"Mama, I don't *ever* intend to have sex. And as for drugs, forget it. I'm not stupid, you know."

"I know you're not, sweetie. It would just help me to know I had your word for it—no drugs or sex while you're in high school."

"This is junior high."

"Same difference."

"Okay, no drugs or sex. God, I can't believe this."

"If anything *does* happen, Edda, I want you to talk to me about it. That's very important. Anything at all, I'm here."

"Okay. I'm going to be late if I don't get going. Any other words of warning?" I was absolutely dripping with sarcasm, all of which was lost on her.

She thought for a moment. "Well, just take care of yourself and act normal. You know."

I had to laugh. My mother telling *me* to act normal. That's just about all I ever did. I was becoming a master at it. What I wished was that *she* would try it too. Act normal. I thought Mama didn't fit in in Spence because she wasn't from Spence. I thought that once we moved, something big would change, in her, in me. But it didn't.

Even in Lexington, a town big enough to have black people, Indians, Orientals, Hispanics, transvestites, and punks—Spence had none of these—even here I could tell Mama was different. Other women didn't talk as much or as fast as she did (that is, when she wasn't silent); they didn't cry or laugh over nothing in particular; they didn't tell their children to act normal, like it was a coat that could be taken on or off. They *were* normal. I began to see that what separated Mama from other people was something in *her*. And at that time I believed that what separated *me* was being her daughter—to my everlasting mortification.

Chandler Junior High was a jungle. There were more kids in those three grades than there had been in all of Spence put together. For the first time I locked my locker with a combination lock, and for the first time I was robbed, repeatedly. Not that I had much for them to take: sneakers one time, a watch, a new notebook, my Cliffs Notes on *The Odyssey*. It happened to everybody; I wasn't being picked on, but I wasn't used to it. I wasn't used to hearing kids cuss so much either, even right to the teachers sometimes. Or the fights. If I had made myself a small but daring reputation in Spence, it was nothing compared to what I saw every day at Chandler. I'm talking about knives and chains in school, tough guys. I spent a lot of time there with my head down, pushing through the crowded halls, trying not to accidentally offend anybody, wishing I were invisible.

Chapter 22

That first year, after several extremely expensive illnesses, our car died. Jimmy and I rode on our first city bus. I remember thinking how amazing it was, the first time we climbed up on one, that here in this noisy, wide interior were fifty other people, going other places.

"Just think," I told Jimmy, "how many people there are in the world."

"How many?" he asked in his ever practical way.

"I don't know. But a lot. So many." I was awed by the sheer numbers of people I was seeing every day, both at school and on the streets. There were so many strangers, so many different faces, so many ways of living, of looking, of dressing, of cutting your hair. . . .

After a while we all got tired of the bus. Many times we got cold and very wet waiting for it to come when it didn't. And in time we all learned to sit face forward, head tipped to the window, with tired, closed faces like everybody else. We were sitting on the bus when I first noticed Mama was going gray. The light was catching in her hair, which was still mostly a shiny black, and I could see all of a sudden how much gray there was. On the bus I would often sit a few seats away from Mama and Jimmy, looking at them and trying to see them as part of the crowd. That's what I was doing when I suddenly realized Mama was going gray.

What she went was salt and pepper. She'd look in the mirror and laugh about it. She told Banker she thought she was getting old. He told her everybody did if they lived long enough. She'd brush out her long, long hair and study the gray. "See how it's more crinkled up than the rest of it, Edda," she'd say. "That's because it's lost its vigor, it's worn out. But I don't care," she'd add, "I like it. It's mine." And she would sit and brush it out. Sometimes I'd braid it for her because her arm still went numb, and she couldn't reach behind her head very well.

I kept my hair cut short or just growing out. Mrs. Stumbo had experimented on me for so many years that I was used to lots of different styles. There was a school of hair design not far from our house; their prices were cut-rate, and I went there for years. Not that it helped. My looks have always been just this side of average and my hair especially. Jimmy had these incredibly thick, golden curls, and Mama had that black-and-white mane, very thick. Banker, of course, had almost no hair at all. Mama said I had hair like Daddy's, and I could tell from looking at the pictures that I did. He and I sort of looked alike, lanky, thin, tall people with fly-away nondescript hair.

I'm glad I look like Daddy, but I wished then (and I still

wouldn't mind) to look more like a girl. One of the main reasons I got my ears pierced in the ninth grade was because it was apparent by then that I was always going to be flat-chested, and I didn't want *ever* to be mistaken for a boy. Mama was horrified when I came home one day with gold studs in. I hadn't told her I was going to do it, had hardly known myself. But a store near school was offering it for five dollars, and I had five dollars, so I did it.

"But, Edda, those are two extra holes in your body, for life!" Mama said when she saw me. She was really upset.

"So what?"

"I just can't imagine doing such a thing to my body. There are enough wounds inflicted and scars to bear as we go along. Why add more? What are you trying to do, get a jump on it?"

"They're not scars, Mama, they're pierced ears." She could blow up the littlest things into major big deals.

"Well, they're the same as scars, they're holes, aren't they? Aren't all those stitches in your knee good enough for you? And what about your little finger? That one's even slightly ornamental." She was referring to childhood injuries. The one on my little finger was from where she (by accident, she swears, and truly I believe her) slammed the back door on my little finger when I was two years old. The stitches never came out right, and it looks like a little face on the inside top part of my baby finger on my left hand. Ornamental, it's not.

"These are *not* scars, they're earrings," I told her angrily, and finally she dropped it. Banker said they looked very nice, which was more like it.

We settled in. I offered my services as a baby-sitter in the neighborhood, and there was plenty of business. I made enough money to support what few habits I possessed. Mama made the honor roll her first semester at school, and we celebrated by walking down the street for pizza. Jimmy made friends with kids in the alley behind the house and learned to play basketball. Banker began walking to the store once a day to pick up his own papers. This delighted Mama, who was forever on him to get out more.

It was on one of those walks that he met Henry John.

Chapter 23

I came home from school that afternoon and found Henry John and Mama sitting in Banker's room. They were holding hands; both were crying. Banker was looking like a priest. I stared. Henry John got up and wiped his eyes. He took my hands and said how much I'd grown. Mama got up too and put her arms around my waist. "See," she said, "Edda's almost taller than me." Which was true. I wriggled loose of her hold, which felt unnaturally tight, and said hello.

Henry John lived on the other side of town from us. He said it was a coincidence (of course, what else?) that he had been in that supermarket near our house just when Banker had come there to buy his paper. We'd lived in Lexington for over a year by then, and I had never much thought, Henry John lives here too somewhere. I knew he did. We all knew that, but I never looked for him. When I did think of him, it was as he was back on Cauley's Creek.

I found out that day, and especially late that night when Mama kept me up late talking to me, that it hadn't been the same for her. She knew he was there and could never stop looking for him, although she tried not to.

That night, after Henry John left, after dinner, after I was up in my room reading, after Jimmy had gone back out in the alley to shoot a few more balls, and after Banker was in bed, Mama came in to talk. I wish she hadn't. I wish she had gone to someone else, someone grown, someone other than her daughter, than me. I wish I'd been able to tell her that too, to do anything but get angry at her. But I couldn't. Suddenly I was unable to bear another confidence of hers. I wanted to be left alone, left out of it. I didn't want to know. I, who'd perfected the lonely art of eavesdropping, no longer wanted to hear. She told me anyway, of course, at least until I got her started on another path, on a fight with me, so she could walk out and slam the door behind her, walk the floor outside my room muttering about teenagers.

But before that, when she burst in on me saying she needed to talk to me, like she was thirteen or I was thirty-three, she gave me no chance to reply.

"Oh God, Edda, I can't believe he was here. God. After so long. So many times, so many times I've looked for him, so many times. And I know it's a sin or at least very wrong, I know that. How many times? Every time we're out. When I'm at the university. Whenever I see a truck like his. You didn't know that, did you? I've thought of him so much." She sat on my bed cross-legged, her long skirt pulled over her knees, and looked small and very cold. She was wearing two sweaters and rubbed her hands together as she talked. The words were racing out. "What goes around comes around, Edda. I always knew there was something to that song. He's a married man, may God forgive me. Forgive me what though? I'm not going to do anything. I'm not. I swear I'm not. I'm going to live with it, live it through. What else can I do?" She started to cry and sat there rubbing her eyes like a little girl. "Why is there love if it feels so bad?" she asked, not of me, I sensed, but of God or the universe in general. It was something sobbed up from deep inside.

I wanted her to go away.

I went to my dresser drawer and took out five bottles of vitamins. The girls at the beauty academy had recommended vitamins for my complexion. I bought them one bottle at a time, at considerable expense, with my own money. Mama had never seen them before. They were my private horde, my stash. She watched me count out pills, piling up my nightly dose. As I knew she would, she came over, asked what they were, picked them up and looked at them, sniffed them, looked at me, and was thus successfully diverted from her misery about love. We began instead a long suspicious volley of questions and answers. When she was finally convinced that they were indeed vitamins, she began a lecture about taking pills. "I don't think you should take so many pills. Even if they are vitamins. It just doesn't seem healthy."

"And I suppose smoking cigarettes *is* healthy?" I asked. I had her in an old familiar corner now.

"I know, I know. But I've told you before, I'm trying.

That's my problem. Don't go trying to turn the tables on me, young lady. I'm talking to you about pill taking."

And so it went until she left the room, slamming the door behind her and standing in the hall, supposedly talking to herself. After an argument was over, finished, she would stand around in the next room or outside the door as she did then, putting on a few finishing touches. Supposedly, she was talking to herself, "What can you expect, Frances?" she'd mumble, fooling no one.

Late, late that night she came back. This time she knocked. I was half asleep, with the light on but dozing, still in my clothes. "Come in?" I said thickly.

"Sweetie, I'm sorry," she said. "I don't want you to go to bed mad. Okay?" She was sitting next to me, stroking hair out of my eyes.

"Okay, Mama. It's okay, I'm not a pill popper, you know. They really are vitamins."

"I know that, and I got to thinking how lucky I am not to have anything worse to worry about than you taking vitamins. I don't know why we fight. It's just like they say in the books about raising teenagers. We fight." She laughed weakly and we were both quiet.

After a while she said, "Edda, I know I shouldn't burden you with this. It's practically none of your business but I just somehow . . ."

I could think of nothing to say, and she too was silent again. At long last she spoke. "I want for you to be happy in love someday. And to have it last. I want this for you. I want it still for myself, although I no longer expect it can be. I really don't. What's happened to me with Henry John, it's just something to be borne. They say the first couple of years after a divorce are full of adjustments."

"Oh Mama. Come on."

"I'm perfectly serious."

"That's what worries me."

In some ways Mama divorcing Daddy had brought him back to life. She talked about him often, referring to him as "your father" to Jimmy and me. It seemed to me she had an unfair advantage as far as knowing his opinions: "Your father would want you to study if you're having trouble in geometry." Or to Jimmy: "Your father loved basketball, but he was above all a good sport, and he would hate to hear about you spitting at someone just because you're in a temper." And sometimes, like she was doing just then, she referred to him as her ex-husband. One time she even introduced herself that way, as an ex-wife. It made my skin crawl.

"You take a patronizing attitude with me about this, Edda, but I know whereof I speak. Divorcing your father was much different than surviving his death. And I think how I turned down Henry, and how now, now it's too late. And it hurts. Okay? That's what I'm saying."

"I know." And I did. Could I pretend not to? She was hurting.

"The other thing I'm trying to get across here is that I

want it better for you. If you can learn from my mistakes, do so."

"Mama, I want to make my own. I want to figure it out for myself."

"Well, of course you do. I was the same way."

And then, as I dozed, she talked. Of love, of pain, of betrayal, of yearning, of scruples, and of hope, which she said could be more terrible than hopelessness. I was too tired to stop her, too tired to distract her with vitamins, too tired almost to listen. But I heard.

Mama needed a friend, a woman friend, someone like Annie, although it would never again be Annie. There would be no more sisters. If she had divorced Daddy, what is it she did to Annie, who was simply cut off, cut out, made null and void? My mother was a woman who knew how to close a door.

Henry John was above all a married man. To Mama, a woman who'd divorced her dead husband for adultery, this meant something. In the weeks that followed he came by several times. In my horrible wisdom I could see all the symptoms. They looked at each other and looked away. They never touched, but there was an electrical current between them so strong as to be dangerous for the poor fool who wandered innocently into its field. Jimmy did that one night, walked up to Mama where she was standing, at the sink. Henry John was beside her, drying dishes. Jimmy had reached out to hug her, to kiss her, I think, and jumped back startled. It was a good thing he was wearing tennis shoes, considering all the water.

192·

And then one night it was over. Over again. Again with a fight that could be heard upstairs. Jimmy came into my room with a scared, puzzled look on his face. "What's going on?" he asked me. Me, as if I knew, which in fact I did. I'd shut my door to their noise, but it came up anyway, through the heating vents, the thin plaster of The Living End, where nothing was ever private for long. Henry John had offered himself to Mama but not in marriage. Simply offered. And she was furious. Is that what moral fiber weaves, a sheltering cape? I could think of no way to explain it to Jimmy, so we played cards instead. And still we listened. It was impossible not to.

So it was that Henry John came back and then was gone again. Mama would be no man's mistress. Not even his. The fact that he had asked it of her helped her give him up. Or so she said. She would never do to another woman what Annie had done to her. There was right and there was wrong. Or so she said. New lines appeared in her face; her mouth drew down, and her jaw set. She cried less and laughed less too. Being right, I deduced, was a grim business.

Chapter 24

It seems that it was no time at all before we saw him again. In fact it was two years. I was in high school. I had learned to wear makeup, to dance, to deal with drunken kisses from the father of some children I baby-sat for. I had joined the debate club at school and held an undistinguished record. Once by then, on my own, I had fallen in and out of love. Jimmy was nine going on nineteen (as Banker used to say). Mama'd caught him trying to smoke cigarettes in the bathroom. The crowd of kids on the alley that he ran with were mostly older and tougher. Some of them stole. Banker had suffered and survived a small heart attack. Mama was almost finished with school, almost a real nurse. She talked about getting a real house and a real job, as if everything she was, was only waiting to be real. There were times she talked to me about love, about being a woman, about men in general, about Daddy, but never Henry John. Had I thought about it, I might have realized that that in itself made his status special.

It was five o'clock on a Saturday morning when Henry

John rang our bell. I heard it but only dimly, through sleep. Mama went downstairs and opened the door to him. He was carrying a baby. It was wintertime; she asked him in.

What did they say to each other? I don't know. It was a conversation I was not privy to—for once, thank God. They settled what there was to be settled between them without my knowing. They let me sleep.

When I came down for breakfast, it must have been 8:30 or 9:00. They were sitting in the kitchen drinking coffee, talking amiably, admiring the baby. There was a fantastical atmosphere of domesticity, as though I had walked onto the set of some TV show and not our own kitchen. There was snow falling outside, and bright sunshine reflected in light jumpy patches around the room.

"Edda, come here and look at this," Mama said, smiling at me as I came, half awake, into this sunny, off-balance scene. Henry John was holding a white bundle of blankets. He too smiled at me, proudly.

Very carefully, he pulled back the blanket. There, sleeping in the sunlight, was a beautiful, pink-cheeked, black-haired baby. "This is Alexandra," Henry John said in a soft, husky voice.

"She's your new sister, Edda," Mama said.

"She is?" I answered dumbly. I looked at her some more.

"Yes. Henry is giving her to us."

I looked at her, at Henry John. They were both smiling still, nodding at me, yes. Yes.

"Is that legal?" I asked. This simple question had obviously not occurred to either one of them. Whatever was settled in the time between 5:00 and 9:00, it was not the legality of it. They both looked stunned.

"I don't know," Mama said, wrinkling her forehead. "Is it, Henry?" She asked this of him as though she asked him things every day.

"Well, come to think of it, I don't know either," he answered. He too spoke as though it was any ordinary question, as though questions and answers were old between them. What do you want for dinner tonight? Well, come to think of it, I don't know. Is it legal for me to give you a baby? Well, come to think of it . . .

"Her mother doesn't want her," Mama said in a voice that sounded thin and strange, a mixture of sad puzzlement and deep delight.

"What?" I asked, awake at last. I looked again at Alexandra. She was very, very young. Two weeks, they told me later. "Why not?" I asked.

Henry John looked at me with his sad brown eyes. "Why not?" I asked again.

"She's not perfect," he said as though this explained it.

"Nobody's perfect," I answered automatically, the words out before I heard them echo back from years ago. "Nobody's perfect," Annie had said to Henry John, meaning you blew up Ed.

Mama laughed. She heard no echo; she'd been out of the room.

"So right you are, my love," she said. "Nobody is perfect.

Or else we all are, just as we are, imperfect. No. How can that make sense? But it's exactly what I think. We are perfect, as is. Messed up. Lousy. Perfect."

"Whose baby is she?" I asked, still trying to figure out the bare essentials. I was not ready for philosophy.

"She's mine," Henry John said. Gently, he pulled the blanket back up, to guard her sleep.

"And?"

"And I'm giving her to Frances. Her mother doesn't want her."

"Who *is* her mother?"

"Emily. My wife." He said this very carefully, as though tasting the words before he spoke them.

"And she doesn't want this baby? It's hers?"

"Right."

"Okay." I felt exhausted by their density. "Why not?"

"Well, it's hard to explain."

"I'm getting that idea."

Just then Ali turned, cried out a little, woke up. We all looked at her. Her eyes were dark, dark blue. They were changing even then to brown. She stared up at us with the solemn, unblinking dignity of the newborn.

"Hi," I said.

"Hi," she said. I swear she did. Henry John and Mama swore it too. We all heard her. It was a totally crystal voice, tiny and pure. "Hi!"

"My God, Henry, she can talk!" Mama said. We all laughed, and brilliant Ali smiled.

"Henry, give her here to me," Mama said, holding out her arms. He handed her the baby, and Mama held her close in a hug that I knew was warm and sweet. I could almost remember being hugged that way myself. "She's wet. I'm going to change her. Edda, see that bag over there? Will you get it for me?" On the floor was a grocery bag with Pampers and bottles and formula, a few changes of clothes, an extra blanket. This was her luggage.

Mama took Ali into the living room and laid her down on the couch. Henry John and I followed. Carefully, she unwrapped the blanket, cooing to her softly. I saw then, kicking out from her little nightgown, her misshapen foot. Her right foot had no toes and almost no bone, or so it seemed. Mama ran her hands over both of Ali's legs and feet. It was a caress.

"So now you see. This is why we get to keep her."

"Because of her foot?" I asked.

"Yes. That's right. It's part of her, but Emily"—Mama said this nodding at Henry John—"can't stand it. It makes her sick."

"Are you kidding?" I kept thinking this was a joke, a put-on. It seemed so strange to be seeing Henry John, for him to have brought a baby, to see Mama so excited.

"No," Henry John answered me, "she's telling you the truth. Emily didn't want a baby at all. Ali was sort of an accident. You know." Was he blushing? "I'm the one who pressed for it, who wanted a child. But when she came out like—like this, it was just more than she could handle. She won't feed her; she lets her lie there and cry. She really doesn't want her." He shrugged his shoulders. I shook my head in disbelief, in wonder, and in a slow dawning comprehension. Mama's head was bent, changing Ali's diaper, but the smile on her face was evident even so.

Chapter 25

Henry John divorced Emily, but he didn't come to live with us. At first he visited on the weekends, like a father who doesn't have custody. He gave us money—lots of it, it seemed to me—to help take care of Ali. That very Saturday, when she first came, he and I sat down at the kitchen table and looked at bills. Jimmy and Banker walked to the store to buy more diapers and formula and brought us the receipts. Mama got on the phone to figure out about a baby-sitter for when she was working or in class.

It seems to me, in memory, that that morning marked the beginning of something. It was as though when I walked into that bright yellow kitchen with its cold floor and bouncing snowy light, with its two beaming grown-ups and one sleeping baby, that a shade was flung up somewhere, a switch was thrown, the sleeping castle came to life. Something like that.

Ali created bustle and noise and work and problems where they hadn't existed before. We had to rearrange schedules, plans, meals. We had to feed her (constantly) and change her diapers, watch out for her when she started to roll over and move around. It seemed we were constantly going places and taking Ali with us. Or she was going places—the doctor's, the baby-sitter's—and we were taking her. Ali was not an easy baby. She didn't sleep much, and although she didn't fuss all the time, when she did fuss it was not to be ignored.

But for all the trouble she created, she was worth it. Call it love; we loved her. Even as a tiny thing she radiated energy. I've never known anyone more interested in people. We never heard her say "hi" again until she was a year old, but when anyone talked to her or held her, she paid attention to them like she understood. She was an intelligent listener. And when she finally learned to crawl, it was always toward a person's leg, to pull up on it and look them deeply in the face. She was a long time learning to crawl, even longer learning to walk. Her misshapen foot threw her off balance, but she eventually developed a lopsided lope that took her anywhere she wanted to go. Surgery was discussed and eventually ruled out. Instead, the doctors fitted her with some ugly brown orthopedic shoes, which Mama immediately painted pink and green and yellow.

When Mama graduated from nursing school, she took a part-time job at an institution for retarded adults. This was instead of the full-time job she'd had promised to her at a hospital. She wanted time to be with Ali and to be home more with Jimmy. The money was about the same as she'd made as a typist, but she was a real nurse at last and far away from the emergency rooms that I still dreaded. She quit smoking and started crying again. And laughing. It was good to see her leaking and weeping again. Her juices were running. Happy or sad, she cried and laughed. Before Ali she'd begun to acquire a dried-out, withered look, which then began to fade. Or fill in. She was tired a lot and had big circles under her eyes, which she covered with makeup. But essentially, deep down, she was in good shape. She was being healed.

For her thirty-sixth birthday Henry John gave Mama a car. Just like that. He'd divorced Emily and she him. She'd gone off to dance with a group in San Francisco, and he'd sold their house and moved into an apartment. It was with this house money that he took Mama out and bought her a car. A new car. A blue Datsun station wagon. Stick shift. When I got my driver's permit, she took me to the Lexington Cemetery and taught me how to drive. She said she chose the cemetery because there wasn't a lot of traffic and there were hills, so that I could practice starting on hills. I think also she wanted the silent reminder of mortality with me behind the wheel. Accidents can happen. She knew it well. We all did.

Henry John courted Mama openly, almost ridiculously, on the weekends. He made up songs for her, brought her flowers and bottles of whiskey and candy. Anything broken he fixed. Every six months, rain or shine, he asked her for her hand in marriage. She refused him, but they stayed on good terms. She'd say she couldn't trust him, say she wasn't ready, wasn't sure. Because he'd propositioned her while he was married to Emily, he was, she thought, likely to do the same to someone else if he was married to her. Henry John would swear it wasn't so, and she'd say, "But how can I be sure?" Then they'd drop it for another six months. It was a little dance they did, almost like a joke. Except it wasn't. There was something pathetic about it, and romantic. Is that a contradiction?

After one of these go-rounds, Jimmy announced he was never going to get married—period. First of all, he intended to be a detective after he finished with his career in pro sports, so he wouldn't have time, and second of all, he said, why go to so much trouble just to get divorced? I could see his point. It seemed like everyone we knew was divorced. Except Banker, and he had never married. Mama would tell Jimmy not to get cynical, that there are good marriages, that it is possible, that even marriages that don't last, like hers to Daddy, have good times in them, beautiful times. But Jimmy said he would never do it. He was sour on it.

Once we were invited to a wedding at the place where Mama worked. Two of the inmates were getting married. It wasn't encouraged, but these two people had managed it. We all went. The wedding was held in the institution's cafeteria, which had been hung with bright crepe paper. Mama cried, of course, and kissed and hugged a lot of people we didn't know.

On the way home she said, "Wasn't it beautiful?"

"Very nice, very nice," Banker agreed.

Jimmy said, "Maybe being retarded helps."

"Maybe so," Mama answered with a smile at Henry John.

Such was their courtship, if that's the right word for it. How long they would have gone on like that is untelling.

The person who, in my opinion, actually put an end to all this was Emily. She showed up one day without warning. We were at dinner—Ali, Jimmy, and I. Mama was not there. Emily knocked on the back door, and I opened it casually, thinking it was somebody from next door wanting to use our phone.

"Oh," I said in surprise, when I realized I didn't know this woman. "Yes?"

"I'm Emily," she said. It didn't mean anything at first to any of us. "Alexandra's mother." She was staring at Ali—Alexandra—who was sitting in her high chair, playing with green beans.

"Mama's not here," Ali said in her little croaky voice. "Out. But she'll be back," she sing-songed. This was the chant we used to soothe her with when Mama had to leave. She'soutbutshe'llbeback.

"Come in," Jimmy said. He was the only one of us who had any real manners.

What impressed me most about Emily was how ordinary she was. I'd expected someone strange—beautiful and wicked and wild. I thought all dancers were very tall, but I was taller than Emily. And women who gave up their children—I'm not sure what I thought they'd look like. But not like this. She wore jeans and a white shirt. Very plain, no jewelry or makeup. Her short brown hair was cut close around her head in a Prince Valiant style, and her eyes were brown. Kind. Yes, she had kind eyes. How could she?

I thought first of running to Banker's room, to rouse him, tell him what was going on (what was going on?), get him to help. I was seventeen years old and officially in charge. Should I call the police? I imagined wrestling her down, pushing her out of the house, locking the door. It would be simple. Jimmy offered her something to drink. "We have milk, orange juice, beer, and water," he said, looking into the refrigerator. "And we could make you some coffee," he added, raising his eyebrows at me for confirmation. I nodded yes. I supposed I could make her some coffee. She took a beer.

"I know you wonder why I'm here," Emily said, addressing me. Oh yes, I wondered. All three of us looked at her, waiting. What did we look like to her?

"I just wanted to see her. That's all. Just see her." Emily spoke in a quiet, calm voice. "See all of you. It's been two years. I'm not going to take her, if that's what you're worried about. Honest," she added when she saw I was still staring, still sizing her up.

So she wanted to look. Okay, she could look. I even let her touch, let her hold Ali on her lap. It was hard to realize that this was Ali's mother. She seemed so innocent.

Chapter 26

So Ali has two mothers. Emily, who comes to look, and Mama who is with her all the time. She is now seven years old and doesn't seem confused about it. I don't know what she will think of it later, but for now it seems a natural part of her life, like losing teeth and having new ones grow in. She clunks around on her fat shoes and tiny foot. Sometimes she cries when she can't keep up with her friends, but mostly she is happy, happy-natured. Mama and Emily are not friends and not enemies. I suppose they are some kind of kin to each other. As I am, as we all are to each other in different ways. Henry John and Mama are now husband and wife. Have been for five years. From what I can see, they are happy. May they live in peace.

I don't live with them anymore. After they got married, we moved. It was to a nice big house, all ours. I settled up with Mr. X for old bills. Over the years he and I had developed a friendly business relationship. The day we moved he came over to see us off. It was unusual for him to come to the house at all. One by one, he shook everybody's hand, starting with me. It was very formal, a gesture from an old world.

Emily stayed around for two days that first time. After that she'd pop in and out at different intervals. Never for very long, and she never stayed with us. She'd just come over and hang around for a while—an hour or two, a day or two, never longer. She'd look at Ali, talk to her, talk to us, look at us. And then she'd leave. She had places to go. It was hard for me to realize that there was nothing particularly despicable about Emily. Before I knew her I assumed there was something wrong with her because she didn't want Ali. Who could not want Ali? I thought Emily was unnatural, but she's not. She's a regular person. And Mama *did* want Ali; we all did, and we got her, thanks to Emily not wanting her and to Henry John for giving her to us. (By the grace of God is what Banker said it was. And he was right.) Ali is a blessing.

That very first night they met Emily told Mama that she was a fool not to marry Henry John. I had come downstairs to brush my teeth. It was late. I was in my nightgown and bare feet. They were in the kitchen, still talking. That's what she said: "Frances, you're a fool not to marry him. You two are perfect for each other. We weren't. That's all, no hard feelings."

"Well, I'll think about it" is what Mama replied.

She didn't think long. They were married three weeks later, the same week I graduated from high school. They moved the day after they were married, and I went off to school after that. I was glad to get away.

For four years I went to college in the Midwest. I visited them on vacations, saw them in the summer some. I've seen Jimmy going through high school in a completely different way than I did. He's got friends. He plays sports. People know him. I had remained a loner. The day I finished my senior finals I walked along Main Street and put nickels into every parking meter on the street. It was all I could think of to do for a celebration. I was getting out and felt generous, lucky, but with no one to share it.

In college I studied around: journalism, education, psychology, and physics. I couldn't settle down. I tried to make friends and did make a few. I finally graduated with a degree in liberal arts, equipped to do very little but to think about what little I did. Do. That's what I'm doing now. Very little. I need a rest.

Last year, after I graduated, Charlie Henson sent me a letter. Charlie, from Spence. His family is still there. Charlie had gone on scholarship to M.I.T. He works now for a computer corporation outside of Washington, D.C., and I live in this beach house that belongs to a friend of his. He lives with me too sometimes, when he can get away. I've been here since September. It is now February. In May I have to leave. In the meantime I sit and watch the ocean. I am resting from my childhood.

Charlie took me back to Spence for a weekend before we left to come out here. We visited with his family and saw Mrs. Stumbo, who did get a baby, two. Amy Eversole is married (not to Bill Peyton) and pregnant. Our old house on Cauley's Creek has burned down, and a trailer is there now. We didn't get out and cross the creek to go to Heaven. If they don't strip-mine too close to it, Heaven will always be there. Annie's house is still standing, but Charlie didn't know if she lived there still or not. Her Jeep was gone, and the house had an empty look to it. I didn't go up on the porch or knock or leave a note, just drove by. The last day we walked up to my father's grave. I said hello. Good-bye. What do you say to a grave?

Mama writes and gives me news. All is well. For now. She sends love. Says she envies me the ocean. Jimmy writes too, occasionally. I miss him very much sometimes. He made the basketball team this year. Last week Ali had a dream that she was dancing and woke up crying. It made me sad to hear that. Henry John and Mama have taken up horseback riding together. It seems funny to think of them out riding around on the hills in the bluegrass, but that's what they do with their spare time.

I sit and think and watch the ocean. When I get up, it will be my turn to be a grown-up, an adult. I'll get a job and do something. Meanwhile I sit and think and watch the ocean. And I love Charlie. So I wonder about that. What will come of it. What has come of it already?

Mama walked off from the people who raised her and never looked back. I don't want to do that. But I do want to be free of them, want them in perspective, want myself apart. I need to shake them loose, let go. Charlie says everybody has to raise their parents. Is that true? He says the time comes for all of us when we have to kiss them good-bye and trust them to be okay on their own. I've done the best I could with mine. Good-bye, you all, and good luck. Good-bye and keep cold.